SILENCE SAYS THE MOST

SILENCE SAYS THE MOST

An Olivia Penn Mystery

THE OLIVIA PENN MYSTERY SERIES
BOOK II

KATHLEEN BAILEY

First hardcover edition: October 2022
First paperback edition: October 2022

ISBN (hardcover): 978-1-956270-06-8
ISBN (paperback): 978-1-956270-05-1
ISBN (e-book): 978-1-956270-04-4

Editing by Serena Clarke at Free Bird Editing
Proofreading by LaVerne Clark at LaVerne Clark Editing
Cover design by Robin Vuchnich at My Custom Book Cover

Published by:
Rhino Publishing LLC
P.O. Box 295
Fairfax, VA 22038-0295

www.kathleenbaileyauthor.com

For my Dad

Saying nothing … sometimes says the most.

— EMILY DICKINSON

CHAPTER 1

Olivia Penn scanned the serene, dark water of Lake Crystal and imagined floating, allowing the surface tension to conform to her body like memory foam. This time last year, she had probably been hustling to grab a pastry and a double shot of espresso for a quick lunch with work colleagues in Georgetown. Routines had regimented her days, and flow charts had depicted her daily schedules. So much had changed.

She had returned to her hometown of Apple Station, Virginia, five months ago to visit her father before a planned relocation to New York. That life seemed distant now. She had eased into days such as this without regret or difficulty. Though her long-term plans still were unclear, she felt more like herself than she had for some time.

Buddy, her father's beagle puppy, ambled close by her side, secured by a red leash dangling casually from her fingertips. She and her forever friend A.J. had finished their picnic lunch and were walking around the lakefront back to her Expedition to pack up and return to their respective workdays. Inseparable in childhood and now in their thirties, she and A.J. had grown up as neighbors. Each was an only child, and they had become like siblings. A.J. was tall and athletic, and when they were kids, he always encouraged her to tag along when he met with his schoolmates to play pick-up games of soccer and football on the town square. Her agility and quick-thinking made her an asset, regardless of the sport, and she often was selected as a team member even before some of A.J.'s slightly older friends. Now, instead of playing games, they fueled their friendship with these occasional noontime Monday lunch excursions. They always tried to eat outside, but as fall had swept in, the coming, cooler winter days soon would keep their catch-up sessions to cozier confines.

Lake Crystal State Park was located twenty minutes from the heart of Apple Station. The eponymous lake was expansive and accessed from the park's front side by a trail that cut through woodland. The lake, though, wasn't visible from the entrance, where the playground, pavilions, and picnic tables were more conveniently staged. Dense forest filled with yellow poplar, white oak, and red maple trees separated the areas and isolated the lake.

On weekends, there was a constant back-and-forth flow of visitors from the lot to the lake, but on this crisp

Monday afternoon, she and A.J. had the park mostly to themselves. The only other person they had even noticed was a man standing at the end of a nearby dock, inspecting the kayak launch port.

The dock had been a fixture for as long as Olivia could remember. As a child, she was among the fearless who used the thirty-yard platform as a runway to generate speed and cannonball into the lake. She and A.J. would dash down the dock, holding hands while counting the seconds to their daring leaps. The dock lacked guards or rails, and it had seen better days. Worn, horizontal slats of pressure-treated pine creaked and moaned on their own, even without applied weight. Some wanted it removed, others wanted it replaced. Patchwork repairs, though, were the best the park authority's budget could do, and so it remained.

Buddy sniffed his way to the water's edge. Olivia loosened her hold on the leash, letting out some slack and allowing him to linger, as she was in no hurry to get back to writing for her advice column. When she had worked at her office in Washington, D.C., she had been hyper-efficient in churning out her columns. She could sit for hours tapping away on her keyboard, unaware of how much time had passed until her body grumbled, protesting with an achy neck and a tired, sore back. Now that she was working remotely, there always seemed to be a distraction.

A.J. set the tote bag containing their trash and lunch wares on the ground and then grabbed a smooth stone about half the size of a clementine from the shore's edge. He reeled his arm back and slung the stone fast and low toward the lake's surface. Skip-skip-skip-skip.

"You were always pretty good at that," Olivia said.

He offered a theatrical bow. "I would challenge you to a duel, but it wouldn't be sporting of me to take advantage of your frail arm. I'm sure you're still rusty from the break."

She playfully bristled at his faux chivalry and switched the leash to her left hand. "My wrist is right as rain, stronger than ever. I pity the fool who thinks otherwise. Game on." She selected a perfect triangular stone, about the size of her palm. "Don't say I didn't warn you." She drew her arm back and flung the stone as hard as she could. Skip-skip.

A.J. applauded her with an encouraging, *Rudy*-inspired slow clap. "Bravo, bravo." He haphazardly plucked another stone from the shore and slung it, repeating his performance, while adding a bonus skip for flair.

"I give up," she said. "I concede you're a better rock skipper. Congratulations."

"I want that recorded, so I can make it your ringtone."

She lightly shoved his shoulder. "Sometimes, you're extremely strange."

Buddy was minding his business, uninterested in the playful competition between two of his best friends. The man on the dock tested the kayak lift, cranking the handle, and then walked back toward the shore, stopping every few feet to take pictures of the water with his cell. A slight breeze rustled the treetops, and a flurry of crimson, yellow, and orange leaves fluttered to the ground. Soon, decay would litter the trail through the forest, the beauty of the fall colors fading as the leaves dried and died.

"I can't believe Halloween is on Friday," she said.

A.J. nodded. "You remember that time when we were kids, and we went trick-or-treating dressed as Bonnie and Clyde?"

"How could I forget? Nobody got it."

"We definitely looked more like newsies than gangsters," he said.

The man who had been on the dock walked past them, smiling politely as they exchanged cursory hellos.

"I love everything about fall," A.J. said. "Pumpkin pie, thanksgiving, pecan pie, hot cider, apple pie."

"I'm sensing a theme. It sure doesn't smell like any of those things here. What's that stench?"

"Dead fish." A.J. pointed to where Buddy was standing, staring at five fish floating on their sides. "There's a bloom starting."

She stepped closer to the lake's edge as Buddy ceded his front row view of the crime scene. "Algae? I don't remember that happening here before."

"That's because you haven't lived here for the past ten years. Blooms pop up, especially in the summer when the water is warm. There was one in Lake Anna in August."

Olivia steered Buddy away from the edge. "Let's get away from there, little guy." She reached into the tote bag's side pocket and retrieved his favorite red ball. Buddy vigorously wagged his tail and barked, noting his approval for what she had in mind. She unclipped his leash, stood tall, cocked her arm back, and faked tossing the ball toward the trail through the trees. Buddy's eyes tracked the flight path the ball should've taken, but he didn't budge. She squatted, hiding his toy behind her back, and rubbed under his chin. "Where'd it go? Did you see it?"

He barked again, and she revealed the ball. "Look what I found." She stood and threw it for real this time, clear to the forest line.

"I bet that's why that guy is here," A.J. said.

She brushed her hands on her quick-dry hiking pants, wiping off Buddy's slobber that had transferred from the ball. "The one who passed us?"

"Yeah. Did you notice his jacket?"

"It was really bright yellow."

He shook his head. "You're a regular Nancy Drew. I meant the insignia, VDEQ."

She coiled Buddy's leash and stuffed it into her back pocket. "Should that mean something to me?"

"Virginia Department of Environmental Quality. In September, Whispering Meadows Country Club hired me to install silt fencing around several project sites. They were upgrading the clubhouse and doing underground maintenance work on several of the fairways. Before I could start, they had to get permits from that agency." He picked up the tote bag and slung it over his shoulder. "You wanna head back?" he asked.

"Yeah. Let's get away from this stench."

Buddy bounded back toward them as they made their way to the trail leading to the park's front side. The path was only about forty yards long, and years of frequent foot traffic had worn it smooth. Prominent signs on both ends prohibited the passage of motorized vehicles, horses, and bicycles. Buddy lolloped a few feet ahead of them, stopped, and dropped his ball.

She picked it up and glanced behind her. "Last one, Buddy. Make it count." She threw the ball back toward the lake side of the trail, and then they kept walking.

"You still want to go with me to visit Mary next week?" A.J. asked.

"Sure. Let me know when."

After A.J. reunited with his aunt last May, he had frequently visited her at the home she shared with her daughter Hope and son-in-law Able. Olivia often accompanied him on the forty-five-minute drive, and sometimes Mary would invite them to Sunday dinners. Olivia had helped A.J. reconnect to his past, and Mary had done the same for her.

They exited the trail and strolled the short distance across the grass to her Expedition. A park ranger's SUV and a white pickup with the VDEQ insignia were the only other vehicles in the lot. The man from the dock had removed his yellow safety jacket and was leaning against his truck and talking on his cell, gesturing as if giving directions to some place that was far off and to his right. A small orange kayak, secured by ropes and bungee cords, protruded from the bed of his truck, and a silver metallic case was perched on the opened tailgate.

Olivia looked back for Buddy, expecting him to be close behind, but he hadn't emerged from the trail. She unlocked the Expedition. "Can you throw that tote inside? Looks like Buddy is goofing off. I'll go get him."

A.J. opened the front passenger side door and tossed the bag on the floor well. "Hold on, Liv. I'm coming with." He slammed the door shut and jogged a few strides to catch up.

Buddy was resting on his hind legs near the opposite end of the trail. "Come on, Buddy," she yelled. "Let's go home." She turned to A.J. and lowered her voice. "How has work been? Not too strange being back in that office?"

"I thought it would be at first, but now that it's my construction company with my name, it feels totally different." Once an underpaid employee of a general contractor, A.J. recently had leased the suite in town that his former boss had used to run his business.

She glanced back at Buddy, who hadn't budged, as a child wearing a red jacket dashed behind him across the clearing.

"Whoa! Did you see that?" she said.

"See what?"

She set off, briskly striding back toward the lake. "A little boy just ran right behind Buddy."

"Where are you going, Liv? I'll go get Buddy. You stay here."

"Did you hear what I just said?"

"Okay. You saw a child. Not quite the eighth wonder of the world. I'm sure he's with someone."

She quickened her pace. "I'm not seeing anyone else, and why was he running?"

A sharp breeze whipped and whirled along the trail, scattering the dead, fallen leaves to and fro across the ground. The treetops bowed, and the weakest branches bent as a gunshot shattered the silence.

CHAPTER 2

Olivia jolted, and Buddy zipped his sight toward the dockside of the trail. She launched forward, sprinting along the path through the trees leading to the lake as he sprung up and dashed out of her view.

"Liv, wait!" A.J. chased her down, catching up as they drew near to the clearing. "Stop-stop-stop! Hold on." He clutched the crook of her elbow and reeled her to an abrupt stop before she ran out unprotected into the open.

"You heard that, right?" she said.

He walked her back a few feet and then let go. "Yeah. That was a shotgun. Not super close, though. Sound amplifies over water. It was probably a hunter."

"I've never seen hunters here before. Why would anyone be shooting around the lake? We've got to see where that kid went."

A.J. nodded. "Okay. I'll go first. Stay back a little."

She shadowed his strides, and as they neared the end

of the trail, Buddy spotted her, spun, and bounded back toward them. She grabbed his leash from her back pocket and clipped it on his collar, taking up the slack and keeping him close. Swiveling, she checked in all directions for any other visitors. "I don't see that kid anywhere. I didn't know you could hunt in the park."

"Only in certain areas and seasons. The Department of Wildlife Resources allows managed deer hunts around the lake's far side. There are no campgrounds or facilities over there. It's all forest."

Buddy suddenly lunged forward, but the shortened leash tugged him back, causing him to rear like an agitated stallion. He barked wildly, pressing against his restraint. She dropped to a knee and corralled him in close to calm him, but his tantrum ramped up as he fought to break free.

"Look. Somebody's coming," A.J. said.

She stood, holding tight to the leash as two men trod past the dock toward them. One was a uniformed park ranger wearing regulation gray and green. He was solid and thick-chested with barreled biceps that appeared chiseled by heavy weights. He carried a small bundle wrapped in a jacket under his arm and strode with an authoritative air. The other man was thinner, almost gaunt. He wore a camouflage hoodie and sported a clean-shaven head with a neatly trimmed, full beard. A shotgun was slung over his shoulder, and he moseyed rather than marched.

"It's okay. It's Kevin Fields. He's a park ranger," A.J.

said. He waited until they were closer, and then waved. "Hey, Kevin."

"A.J.," Kevin replied.

"We were around the front side, and Liv and I heard a gunshot."

Kevin dropped the bloodied bundle he was carrying onto the ground, and a ringtail popped out on impact. "A family flagged me down a couple of hours ago and reported seeing a sketchy-looking raccoon staggering around the campgrounds. This one probably had rabies."

The man in the camo sniffed and grasped the shotgun's strap, tugging it tighter to his back. "I killed the critter."

"You should've left it alone, Jason," Kevin said.

"I saw a child in a red jacket run along the trail," Olivia said. "He seemed to be by himself. Did either of you see him?"

Kevin and Jason looked at each other, and then at some vague point past the dock and toward the forest that lined the dirt and gravel trail around the lake.

Kevin held his hand up to his waist. "About this tall? Brown hair? Real fast?"

"I don't know about the hair, but he was quick and about that tall."

"Sounds like Mikey," Jason said. "I better go check." He turned immediately and hurried back in the direction they had just come from.

Kevin pulled out his cell from his pants pocket and

placed a call. He stared at Jason as he veered from the trail, blazed a shortcut through a patch of thigh-high wildflowers, and walked into the woods leading away from the lake.

He waited several seconds before speaking. "Melissa, is Mikey with you? ... Aha ... I'm down here close to the dock. A woman says she saw a boy in a red jacket running on the trail ... okay ... I know. It's not your fault. Jason's on his way ... sounds good ... I'll check in with you later."

He ended the call and then slipped his cell into his pocket. "That boy is Mikey Barns. He's alright. He's at his home with his mother. You saw where Jason walked through the woods up there. There's a trail that leads up a hill right to the back of Melissa's house."

"She lives in the park?" Olivia asked.

"No. The parkland on this border ends about thirty yards off the lake trail. There's several homes set back in there. When all the leaves are down, you can see the lake from Melissa's place." He rewrapped his jacket around the raccoon and then lifted the bundle, allowing the ring-tail to droop lifelessly. "I've got to get this to the health department for testing."

The three of them walked together along the trail to the park's front side in awkward silence. Buddy kept quiet and close to Olivia's side, peeking back at the bundled raccoon whenever he got a few paces ahead of them.

A.J. cleared his throat. "So, Kevin, how's your brother? I haven't seen him for a while."

"Chris is busy, as always, at the farm. This is the last harvest before my parents finalize the sale, and all the fall festival activities are open daily through Halloween. Of course, there's the wedding coming up, too."

Olivia had visited Fields Farm several times through the years for their various agritainment offerings, but she had never met Kevin or his brother. "Is it legal for someone to carry a shotgun in a state park?" she asked.

Kevin looked at her as if she had posed the silliest question.

A.J. jumped in. "This is my friend, Olivia. She's a newish returnee to the area. She's not a hunter."

"With the right license, you can carry guns. Jason may look a fright, but he's relatively harmless. He lives in a mobile home down the road from Melissa's. He swears he was out hunting squirrels when he came across this raccoon."

"Why would he be doing that?" she asked.

Kevin shrugged his shoulders, keeping a stern face, which she posited was his primary expression. "Dinner, I guess."

She glanced at A.J., who hid a smile and mouthed, "Tastes just like chicken."

Kevin transferred the bundled raccoon to under his other arm. "I'm sure Jason was really hunting turkeys. He bags beyond his permit and sells them. I've never caught him, but I know he does it. He poaches ginseng from the park, too."

"The herb?" A.J. asked.

"It's a root. It's all throughout the forest here, but it's illegal to harvest in most state parks, including this one. He can sell it for anywhere from a few hundred to over a thousand dollars per pound."

They reached the park's front side and veered to opposite ends of the lot. A.J. called after Kevin. "Tell Chris to contact me sometime when he's free. I'd like to buy him a drink and catch up on old times."

Kevin nodded. "Will do." Then he turned and walked toward his SUV.

Now that Kevin and his bloodied bundle were no longer in their company, Buddy strained against his leash, pulling back toward the grass. Olivia yielded some slack, not wanting to hurt him by engaging in a tug of war. He peered toward the trail leading to the lake and dug his claws in, trying to bulldoze his way forward. His efforts jerked her arm and would've ripped the loop handle from her hand had she not had it wrapped around her wrist.

"Buddy, stop that. What's got into you today?" She wiggled his leash, creating sideways squiggles, which always put him in a playful mood.

He faced her and then pivoted an abrupt one-eighty, straining again to break free of his tether. She gently reeled in the leash, and when he had shuffled close enough, she lifted him and held him tight.

"I'm sorry, Buddy. I know you want to stay. We'll come back another day." She carried him to the car as

Kevin was helping the VDEQ fieldworker unload the kayak from his truck's bed.

She settled Buddy in the Expedition's rear compartment as A.J. readied to ride shotgun. Then she slid behind the wheel, closed her door, and started the engine.

"That was a weird lunch," she said. "That guy, Jason … a little on the scary side. Who walks around a public park shooting squirrels and raccoons? Have you ever seen a turkey here before?"

"I have. You need to get out of your writing cave more. But maybe we should change our venue until after hunting season is over."

"Agreed." She backed out, and they left the park, heading toward town.

A.J. fiddled with the satellite radio until he lucked into a station playing Halloween tunes.

"So, how do you know Kevin?" she asked.

"Just through his brother, Chris. We were the same year in high school. You know Fields Farm?"

"Yeah, sure. That's the organic farm off the Snickersville Turnpike. I've been there before."

"His parents own it. I heard something about them wanting to sell it. I guess they're going through with it."

A rusty door creaked, and chains rattled against the backdrop of test-tubes bubbling. A snare drum soloed an eerie beat in quarter time, heralding the opening bars of "The Monster Mash." They immediately dropped the subject, as there was nothing more important at that moment than to sing along as loud and off key as possible.

They arrived back in town around one o'clock. Olivia pulled in front of A.J.'s general contracting business. The suite, several shops down from her best friend Sophia's physical therapy clinic, was an all-in-one home base that served as his office, workshop, and storage facility. He hopped out of the Expedition, and she leaned toward the passenger seat before he closed the door.

"What are your plans for the rest of the day?" she asked.

"I have a couple of calls to make, bills to pay, squirrel recipes to find. What about you?"

"I'm going home to my writing cave to finish some work. Nothing too exciting. Just a quiet afternoon."

CHAPTER 3

After rounding her Expedition into her father's driveway, Olivia parked behind his Escape. She had temporarily moved back into her childhood home to live with him five months ago, after the murder of her close friend Paige. The circumstances and aftermath of the crime had led to a transition in her life, and spending more time with her friends and family had provided her comfort and much-needed connection. The living arrangement suited them both. Her father's health and well-being had improved, and it had afforded her time to recover from a broken wrist and mull over her long-term plans.

She grabbed the tote bag from the passenger-side floor and then let Buddy out of the back. He led the way to the full-length covered porch of the colonial-style home and scampered up the steps, waiting for her to follow. One day last week, the spirit of the spooky season had inspired her to decorate the porch with a jack-o'-lantern and a two-foot-tall skeleton sporting a tuxedo with tails. Buddy knocked over the ghoulish figurine every chance he got, defiantly asserting himself as the resident alpha.

She righted the skeleton, opened the front door, and shooed Buddy inside. Her father, William Penn, was sitting on the couch in the living room with his laptop on his knees.

"Hey, Dad."

He glanced up. "How was lunch? How's A.J?"

"He's doing well. Lunch was fun. A little weird."

"You wouldn't believe how many recipes there are for scrambled eggs," he said. "Some say add milk, others suggest adding water. I came across one on this site here that calls for chives. I never thought of that. We used to grow chives in the garden. There's still a patch growing by the air conditioner."

"Those aren't chives, Dad. They're weeds."

"No, they're not. I'm going to cut some and put them in my eggs one morning this week. Do we have paprika?"

"I'm not sure. I'll look. It would be on the spice rack in the cabinet with the baking stuff." She walked toward the kitchen, patting his shoulder as she passed the sofa.

She slung the tote bag onto the table and unpacked it, throwing out the trash and loading the used food containers in the dishwasher. After checking the spinning spice rack, she filled a stainless-steel thermos with water from a purifying pitcher in the refrigerator, grabbed her office keys from the wall hook, and stood in the open doorway between the rooms.

"We have paprika. Did you see we have two more cucumbers ready to be picked?"

He continued to click and scroll on his laptop. "I saw them. I swear they grew overnight. I never thought of trying a second planting after the summer crop was done. We'll have to do that from now on. I'll pick the cucumbers later when I get those chives."

"They're weeds. Not chives. I'm going out to the office to write for work."

He offered a one-finger wiggly wave without looking up from his screen as a video of Mary Berry making a brioche frangipane apple pudding played.

She went out through the kitchen door and onto the back porch, then detoured around the side of the house to where the air conditioner unit lodged under the crown of a tall oak tree. She kicked the oak's fallen leaves aside, clearing the ground, and then ripped out the weed patch —just in case.

Rather than dump the weeds into the yard waste bin, she decided to put them in the regular trash, gambling that her father wouldn't think to look there. As she walked to the front of the house to throw them out, she waved to her neighbor, Sam, who was raking leaves along the fence that divided their yards. She had already stacked ten lawn bags by her curb, and Olivia knew she wouldn't stop until the job was done.

Sam was a Marine, now part of the active reserve.

Her husband, who was an Army officer, had perished in combat, and she had kept mostly to herself until Olivia moved back. Since then, though, they had become fast friends. Olivia had coerced her into joining in on girls' night out with her best gal pals, Sophia and Tori. The four of them always had a good time, laughing a bit too loud and staying out much too late. Olivia frequently watched Sam's house and gathered her mail whenever she traveled for work, which was often. Sam confided only that she was some sort of security consultant. The sparse and vague job description dissuaded Olivia from pressing for details.

Sam walked across the yard as Olivia threw the weeds into the trash. "Gardening today?" Sam asked.

"Not quite. Looks like you've been at it for a while, though."

Sam removed her buckskin gloves and stashed them in her back pocket. "This time of year, I could be out here every day working."

"I've got to get out here soon to rake our leaves. If you're not traveling this week for work, why don't you meet up with us on Friday for the Halloween festivities on the town square? Soph and Tori will be there."

"Do I have to dress up?"

"Only if you want to. You'd make a convincing member of Spec Ops." She paused, eyeing the golden Marine Corps emblem on Sam's sweatshirt. "Here's a question for you, given your military background. Do you know anything about gun laws in Virginia?"

"Are you looking to carry concealed? Smith and Wesson make some nice .22-caliber models. I have a Ruger pistol you can try. You might find the 9mm Glock unwieldy with those hands."

Olivia dipped her fingertips into her pants pockets. "No. I don't want to carry concealed. I don't want a gun. What's wrong with my hands?"

"Oh. Nothing. So, what about gun laws?"

"There was this weird incident at Lake Crystal this morning." She explained what had happened, including Kevin's nonchalance about Jason shooting squirrels and the rabid raccoon.

"I know it's disconcerting to see someone carry a shotgun in a public park, but the circumstances seem to check out. It's fall firearms season for turkeys, but muzzleloader season for deer isn't for a few days."

"I'll take your word for it. Are you a hunter?"

"Not exactly. This Jason guy seems like somebody you should avoid. You don't go there alone, do you?"

"Usually not."

"If he gives you any trouble, let me know. I'll take care of him."

Olivia gauged her reflection in Sam's mirrored, wraparound sunglasses, deciding it was best not to press about the details of that either. "It's probably just the time of year that has me spooked. You know Apple Station— thrills and chills around every corner, right? Thanks for the advice, though. I know who to come to if I ever want a gun ..."—she couldn't help but to grin at the tease—"that suits my hands. I'll let you get back to your work."

"Roger that," Sam said with a broad smile.

They parted ways, and Olivia strolled out to her office in the backyard. The one-room outbuilding, near the property's rear border, resembled a miniature New England cottage. A winter-white, screened-in front door popped against the office's soothing, cornflower-blue wood siding. She had adopted her mother's writing space as her own after her employer gave her the green light to work remotely. Since moving back, she had spent countless hours, often late into the night, poring through the volumes of binders her mother had left behind of her journals, stories, and poems.

She settled in her chair at the desk, turned on her laptop, and checked her e-mail. Every week, her editor, Angela, curated a list of reader questions for her to answer. Sometimes, Angela was prescriptive in which ones were priorities, but occasionally, Olivia was free to choose. She always wrote more copy than ever made the papers, but the bonus material was useful for filler on slow news days.

Olivia perused Angela's selections and fell into a familiar routine of reflecting, researching, and writing. She directed readers to hotlines and support groups while including a standard disclaimer in one response that her answer wasn't to be taken as legal advice. She drafted and then rewrote her responses when she felt she was too harsh or not harsh enough. After about an hour and a half, her stomach grumbled, and her thermos ran dry.

She left the office and walked back to the house, entering through the kitchen. Buddy scampered in from the living room, jingling his tags and tapping his claws as if he hadn't seen her for weeks.

Her father was sitting at the kitchen table, snacking on a ham sandwich while tackling his daily crossword puzzle from the newspaper. "Your outing to the park riled him up. He hasn't sat still since you returned. When he gets like this, you just need to take him outside for a game of fetch. I couldn't find his red ball, though."

"He's got to have at least ten balls lying around here." She pointed to the cozy, memory-foam dog bed in the corner of the kitchen. "There's two right in there."

"I know, but he wants his red one. He won't play with the others."

Buddy lapped water from his bowl and then grabbed a red bone-shaped toy with his mouth, letting loose a rapid succession of high-pitched squeaks. She wrestled the toy from him. "Is this new?"

"It was on sale, and I got an additional ten percent off because I'm a senior. See, watch this." Her father stood and retrieved the two balls from the dog bed. He held a blue spiky ball in front of Buddy's nose, and then he rolled it into the living room. "Fetch, Buddy. Go on. Go."

Buddy sat on his hind legs and yawned.

He performed a second trial, bouncing the green ball

to spark more interest, but Buddy expressed the same apathy. "Now, you toss that bone into the living room."

She lobbed the toy, and Buddy chased after it, returning to the kitchen in a snap, squeaking merrily all the way.

"Wow, Dad. Now that's science." She bent forward and coerced the toy from him. "And this thing is annoying. You shouldn't get him used to playing fetch with it. I had his ball with me at the lake. I probably left it in the car. I'll go check. Come on, Buddy."

She grabbed her keys and then went out the back door and around the garden to the driveway. She opened her Expedition's rear compartment and rummaged about. Buddy placed his forepaws on her calves, as if wanting to join in the search. "Down, boy. We're not going anywhere." She checked under the front seats, where everything seemed to fall, but the ball was nowhere. She did, though, find the lip balm she had dropped last week, along with a quarter, two dimes, and a nickel.

"Sorry, little fellow. I don't know where it went. Let's go back inside." She reentered the house through the front door and met her father as he was coming down the stairs. Buddy ignored them both and pranced into the kitchen.

"Was it out there?" her father asked.

"No. I couldn't find it. I may have accidentally left it at the lake. When we were leaving, we ran into someone A.J. knows, and we talked with him for a few minutes.

Buddy was playing with it then, but he must've left it behind. I don't remember packing it up with him."

Buddy trotted back into the living room, squeaking his toy, and then climbed onto the couch.

"Can you run out to the lake and check?" her father asked.

"Now? You're kidding, right? For a two-dollar toy? That would be like finding a needle in a haystack."

Buddy perched on the armrest, judging the distance for a leap to the coffee table.

"It would only take you twenty minutes. Just do a quick look around. He's going to be like this for the rest of the day."

"I was—I am working. I just came in for a bite to eat. I'll order a new one, a red one. We can get it delivered by tomorrow. Or I can run into town later and pick one up at Paws and Claws."

"Do you remember when you were ten, at the start of the school year, on class picture day? You wanted to wear your favorite blue necklace."

"It was turquoise. A.J. gave me that."

"I recall on that morning you couldn't find it, and you refused to go to school for your picture without it. Your mother and I had to search all over this house until we finally found it. Then, we had to call the school and beg the photographer not to leave because you were still coming in for your picture."

"Okay. Perhaps I was being dramatic. But I was ten, and that was my favorite necklace."

Buddy climbed onto the back of the couch, balancing perilously with his forepaws touching and his hind legs shuffling to keep himself from slipping. She caught him before he fell and then placed him on the floor.

"Buddy doesn't have a favorite blue necklace. He has a favorite red ball. Just a quick look, and if you can't find it, then you can order a new one."

She looked down at Buddy as he stared up at her with his soulful, glacier-blue eyes. "Dad, there's no way I'll be able to find it, if it's even there."

He grabbed his fleece jacket from the arm of his recliner. "Okay. I'll run out there and look for it by myself. Hopefully, my heart holds out. There's a lot of ground to cover, but I'll manage. If something happens to me, do you remember where the water shut-off valve is? And your truck needs an oil change. Probably should get the tires rotated and balanced, too. Do that at least once a year. And don't plan anything fancy for me, just a simple service at the church. I have one nice suit—"

"Okay, stop." She shook her head and sighed. "Fine. I'll go. I'll find his ball." She grabbed one of Buddy's leashes from an end table by the steps. "Come on, fur baby. You're with me. We have ourselves a mission."

CHAPTER 4

Olivia drove to Lake Crystal, chiding herself for not noticing the missing ball before leaving the park earlier today. Returning to the scene for a two-bit toy seemed silly, but she did it for her father because he would've come, and she would've followed him anyway. She flipped on the radio, scanning for something up-tempo, and settled on a bluegrass station. An upright bass laid down a racing beat as a banjo and mandolin took turns improvising the melody. She drummed her thumbs on the wheel and hummed along, cheering herself to make the most of this wild-goose chase.

The dashboard's center display console lit with an incoming call as her best friend's ringtone, "Girls Just Want to Have Fun," played through the speakers. She tapped the screen and answered the call hands-free.

"Hey, Soph. What's up?"

"It sounds like you're driving."

"I am. I'm on my way to Lake Crystal. I'm almost there."

"A.J. told me you two were going out there today. Isn't it a little late for lunch?"

"We already came and went. It's a long story." She turned onto the gravel lane leading to the lake's parking lot.

"I was calling to remind you about dinner. FYI, my grandmother is still on the fence about Preston. She's been asking me about the situation, and you're likely to get grilled about it tonight."

She shook her head, slowing as a squirrel scurried across the road. "Please tell her that there's no fence to be on because there is no situation."

"I know that. But after seeing the two of you all cozy at the spring festival in May, she thinks you and him are a thing."

"How does she come to that conclusion? That was over five months ago. I was sitting beside him in a wonky rental chair, eating barbecue chicken and potato salad with a plastic spork because his mother invited me and my dad. There wasn't anything cozy about it. We pass each other occasionally in town, and that's it."

"What about him fixing that side railing on your dad's porch?"

"What about it? He was being nice. A.J. was there, too. Is he also on Josefina's radar for me? There's absolutely nothing there. Nothing to see. Move along."

"Is that nothing for now or nothing forever?"

She rounded the access road's last bend and entered the parking lot. "What time is dinner?"

"It's been over six months since Daniel. Don't you think you should get back into circulation?"

"Daniel who? You're sounding more like Tori every day. Let's talk about you. Remind me, who are you dating? His name is right on the tip of my tongue. Oh wait, sorry. He doesn't exist because you've sworn to stay single and refuse to commit to a long-term relationship. Don't think I won't hesitate to bring that up tonight in front of your grandmother."

"Dinner is at six. Next client is here. Gotta go."

The console display returned to its normal screen after the call disconnected. "Yeah, I thought so."

The VDEQ fieldworker's white pickup was the lone vehicle in the lot. She parked, and then let Buddy out of the back. It was almost three o'clock, and thick, gray clouds had overtaken the day's earlier autumnal blue sky. The temperature had dropped by only a few degrees, but the air shaded chilly. Canadian geese flew in a V formation overhead, honking and heading for cozier environs. She grabbed a zip-up hoodie that she always kept stashed in the backseat and tied it around her waist.

Since no one else was around, she let Buddy roam free. She hoped he would know why they had come and would lead her straight away to his lost toy so she could be back in her office working by four. Perhaps, though, she conceded, this was too much to expect from a puppy.

She locked her car and then secured her keys and Buddy's leash in the hoodie's zip pockets.

Buddy galloped blithely back and forth across the shamrock-green grass. He twirled a few times, chasing his tail, and then followed the meandering flight of a monarch butterfly. She half expected Julie Andrews to emerge from the trail with her arms held wide, singing "The Hills are Alive." Buddy wandered over to the covered pavilion and sniffed under the tables for any morsels that may have fallen from a picnicker's plate. *I don't think he's looking for his ball. I don't think he cares. I don't think dogs can even see red.* A toad hopped along the ground next to him, and he stalked after it. Toad hopped. Buddy hopped. *Why am I even here?*

She set out on her own, letting Buddy play, and hoped that the von Trapp children or Bambi would appear to help put a bow on his day. She reversed the line she had walked with A.J. and Kevin along the park's front side. It would've been too easy for Buddy to have lost his ball out in the open, easily spotted and retrieved. She glanced back at the dog, who was standing near the playground swings and staring at her as if wondering why she wasn't hopping after the toad.

She turned and waved him on. "Are you coming?"

He dashed in no time to her side, and they hiked along the trail between the trees leading to the lake. She scoured the left edge underbrush as they made their way, remembering Buddy had kept to her right on the walk back from the lake. Sturdy, thick oaks grounded by widespread roots towered seventy feet high. Their arching canopies shaded the flora below, aiding all that lived without light to thrive. Small seedlings, fallen from parent trees, had grown wispy trunks in the shadows that bent with every breeze.

"Well, little guy. I don't think it's anywhere back in there. We'll take one quick look around the lake."

When they came into the clearing, Buddy picked up a scent and sniffed along the ground. "Yeah, Buddy. There you go. Find your ball. Where's your red ball?"

He led her off the trail to the water's edge in front of the dead fish—still putrid as week-old garbage. The algae had coalesced around the carcasses, engulfing them in a toxic-green bloom. She pulled him back by his collar. "Get away from there. Come on."

He followed her along the trail as she walked halfway to the dock, scanning the ground and overgrown grass. She glanced behind one last time and then placed her hands on her hips. "Sorry, fella. I think it's gone. We'll stop by Paws and Claws on the way home and buy you a new one. You need a shampoo anyway after being here twice today."

Buddy's body turned rigid as his eyes locked on the dock. He alerted, tipping his tail and barking with a steady, aggressive cadence. She traced his gaze and then peered toward where Jason had entered the forest on the trail leading to Melissa's house. They were alone, and all was serene except for Buddy. She lowered to a knee and stroked his back, soothing him until he stilled.

An osprey glided gracefully overhead, circling and searching for prey. She stood slowly, scanning again while listening for any oddities. The osprey suddenly swooped toward the water with its talons primed to strike. It locked on its target, revved up, and dove in for the kill. In a blink, it spread its powerful wings and soared away, clenching its next meal. The lake splashed in its wake, rippling gentle waves across the surface that bobbed an orange kayak tucked in close by the dock. Buddy meandered ahead on the trail and then looked back and barked, beckoning her to follow.

Despite the lake's open expanse, she felt like she was in a locked room. The trail through the forest was her way in and out, and she was on the wrong side of the funnel. Buddy sauntered out onto the dock, and she stayed close behind. He hated being wet, but it would be just like his mischievous self to leap into the lake when she least expected.

The dock's wood planks were weathered and worn, and several wobbled as she stepped on them. The boards' bending jogged raw memories, triggering her to tense and proceed cautiously. Buddy stood at the end of the dock, peering over the edge.

"Come back, Buddy. Let's go." She glanced behind her as a brisk breeze blew through, scattering a flurry of falling leaves. The launch lift was in the down position, with the kayak primed for entering. "What are you looking at, Buddy?"

She tentatively paced to the edge and peeked over. A

body was floating, snagged to the deck ladder by a yellow jacket. She hit the deck and reached down, desperately grabbing for the collar of the jacket. She tugged to tip the man back, but her grip slipped, and he remained facedown. She popped up and untied her sweatshirt, letting it drop to the dock. Off came her socks and shoes, and then she scurried down three rungs of the ladder and into the water to her waist while keeping one hand glued to the side rail. She threaded one of her legs through two rungs to brace herself. With both hands momentarily free, she grasped his jacket and tilted his head back. A narrow trail of blood from a cut on his head streamed over his cheek and down to his chin. She frantically checked his neck for a pulse, but there was no doubt and nothing she could do. The VDEQ fieldworker was dead.

CHAPTER 5

Olivia's rash attempt to save the stranger hadn't changed his fate, but it did cut loose the tenuous snag that had kept his body from sinking. She clung to the ladder and wrapped her arm around his waist, preventing him from going under. Hauling him up onto the dock wasn't an option as she lacked the strength for that. She could swim him back to shore, but that may tamper with a potential crime scene and destroy physical evidence. Instead, she heaved the VDEQ fieldworker closer to the dock and MacGyvered him. Rigor mortis hadn't set in, so she hooked his right arm over a rung above the water's surface. She threaded his right foot through two lower rungs and then let go. The body stayed as staged. It was the best she could do.

She deftly climbed the ladder, careful not to disturb the precarious positioning. Once back on the dock, a raw chill seized her core, and she shivered from deep within.

Puddles pooled wherever she stepped, and her clothing adhered to her as if shrink-wrapped. She grabbed her socks and sweatshirt and then slipped into her shoes. Buddy stood on the shoreline at the end of the dock and barked as she sprinted toward him.

She hit the shore without stopping and raced back to the park's front side to call the police. The cool, dry air labored her breathing and irritated her throat with each deep inhalation. She hadn't run this fast, this far, for many years. She was a swimmer, not a runner. Slow and steady laps in a pool, not sprints on a track, were her forte. Buddy followed on her heels, and by the time she came into view of the lot, she was spent.

She retrieved her keys from her hoodie's pocket and pressed the remote's unlock button while jogging across the grass. She flung the driver's side door open, tossed her socks and sweatshirt onto the passenger seat, and grabbed her cell from the center console cubby. She dialed the police station's number, and after the third ring, a cool and steady female deputy answered.

"Apple Station police. Deputy Jayden Stone speaking."

Olivia still was trying to catch her breath. "I'm … I'm at Lake Crystal."

"Hold on, ma'am. First, what's your name?"

"Olivia Penn, and there's a dead body in the—"

"Can you spell that for me?"

"My name? There's a dead body here at the lake!"

"Ma'am, please calm down."

"I am calm!" A coughing fit rattled her lungs as her toes were turning numb. Silence reigned until she caught her breath. "Last name is Penn. P-E-double N."

"Thank you, Ms. Penn. Now, you say you found a body at Lake Crystal. Are you sure the individual is deceased, and did you kill said individual?"

"Yes. I mean, no. The deceased is a male, maybe in his thirties. It looks like a drowning, but there's a large gash on his head. He works for the VDEQ. And he's definitely dead. No, I didn't kill him. Why would I have called you if I had?"

"Perhaps to cover up your crime. Classic tactic. Or you could be just plain stupid."

Olivia rubbed her forehead, resorting to the one thing she didn't want to say. "Can I speak to Preston?"

"Detective Hills, you mean?"

"Yeah."

"Hold on," Jayden said. Her voice lowered. "Cole. We've got a dead body at Lake Crystal. Witness on scene. Call Chief Payne and Detective Hills. Ms. Penn, are you still there?"

"Yeah."

"Is anyone else there with you at the lake?"

"I don't think so. I'm in the parking lot now, and there's just my car and his truck. I was here for about ten minutes before I found him. I haven't seen anybody else."

"Okay, thank you for that information, Ms. Penn. Are you in a safe location?"

"I'm by my car."

"Okay. Lock yourself inside and remain on scene until we arrive unless you feel threatened. If you feel you're in danger, vacate the park immediately. We're en route."

The call ended, and Olivia slipped her phone into her pocket. "Buddy! Where are you? Come!"

He sauntered out from behind the Expedition, wagging his tail with a chippy beat and clenching his red ball between his teeth.

"Where did you find that?" She opened the liftgate and hoisted him inside. "Don't you ever lose that again." She grabbed an aluminum softball bat she had stored in the rear compartment ever since last spring, at her father's insistence.

She closed the door and then stood by the hood, keeping her head on a swivel. *It should take twenty minutes for them to get here.* Buddy barked, and she quickstepped to the rear bumper, tightening her grip on the bat. She peered down the access road and into the forest bordering the lot, but there wasn't anything to see or hear that portended a threat. She gently tapped on the window, and Buddy calmed and quieted. "It's okay, little guy. We'll go home soon."

She paced back to the driver's side door and stared at the trail cutting through the forest leading to the lake. *What if the body comes loose and sinks? What if someone else comes across it? What if they have a child with them?* She pulled her keys out of her pocket and clicked the door lock button three times, then took off with the bat in hand toward the lake.

By the time she made it back to the dock, her quick-wicking hiking clothes were semi-dry. *They should be here any minute.* She stood on the shoreline and fixated on the far end of the dock, picturing how she had left the body, half-hugging the ladder as if he had been casually wading in the water. *I should check. I don't want to check. But I should.*

As she stepped onto the dock, her peripheral vision picked up rapid movement. A boy wearing a red sweat-shirt was running on the trail toward her as Jason calmly followed, strolling thirty yards behind.

She rushed to meet the boy before he could get any closer to the dock, but he stopped short of her and veered onto a path leading into the forest. "Hey, wait," she said.

She tightened her grip on the bat, eyeing Jason as he neared. The boy squatted on a narrow trail that cut through a patch of purple asters and knee-high wild grass. He stared at the rough, cracked ground while running his hand back and forth across the dirt. *That must be the way to his house.*

"Hi. It's Mikey, right? I'm Olivia."

He ignored her, focusing on the ground, and then picked up a small stone and examined it closely, turning it every which way. She glanced at Jason, who now was within ten yards. He held onto something slung over his shoulder and was carrying a white plastic grocery bag.

"Mikey. It's okay. You stay here." She stood and squared up to Jason, holding the bat with the barrel out, primed to draw back and swing.

Jason stopped shy of her and flung a dead turkey onto the ground by his feet. He dropped the grocery bag, as if freeing his hands for a fight. "Sorry, miss. You're too late. He's already a goner."

She paced backward and gently lifted Mikey by his elbow, prompting him to stand. "Stay beside me." She pulled out her phone, swiped it open with her thumb, and tapped on her starred contacts. Mikey, though, grabbed the cell and tried to shove her fingers off the screen.

Jason ran his hand over his smooth head and then unzipped his jacket while stepping toward her.

She pocketed her cell and hoisted the bat higher. "Don't come any closer."

A fraught pause accompanied his stare until he casually pulled his phone out of his jacket's inside pocket. He swiped and tapped the screen several times until a bouncy cartoon jingle played. Mikey immediately shuffled over to him and tried to pry the phone away. Jason leaned down and grasped Mikey's index finger to help him touch the screen. A cheerful, recorded female voice spoke. "Mikey, go home." Jason handed him the cell, and then Mikey skipped along the path leading into the trees.

Jason watched until he entered the forest, then turned back to Olivia. "That's augmentative communication.

His speech therapist taught his mother how to use an app on the phone to help him communicate."

"Where's his mother?" she demanded.

"Melissa ran into town. I'm watching him until she returns."

She lowered the bat slightly. "How are you watching him? He was about to run onto the dock." She pointed to the dead turkey. "You're watching him while illegally hunting?"

He bristled and narrowed his eyes. "He knows better than to go out there by himself. What kind of person do you take me for? We were gathering pinecones up by the campground for his art project." He bent forward and tilted the bag toward her, showing off their bounty. "We came across a baited trap in the woods, and this tom was already dead. Fresh kill. Idiots." He spat off to his side. "That's illegal. I busted up their trap, and I took the turkey. They don't get to keep it, but this bird won't go to waste. I told Mikey to walk home while I made sure there weren't any more traps around. I didn't want him to see any other injured or dead animals."

Distant sirens were nearing. "The police will be here soon," she said.

"You called the cops?" He glanced at the path leading into the woods. "Why? Because you thought Mikey was alone?"

She peeked over her shoulder at the dock. "Not exactly."

He leaned forward and picked up the turkey and the

bag of pinecones. "None of it's my business. I should get after Mikey."

She froze, trying to figure out what was happening. On one hand, none of this made sense, but on the other, it kind of did. "The police will want to speak with you." The warning seemed inadequate, like a substitute teacher's threat, but under the circumstances, it was the best she could do.

He nodded and spat again. "It wouldn't be the first time. Tell them I'm at Melissa's." He turned and walked along the path through the wildflowers and into the forest.

She pivoted and paced back toward the dock. *What in the world is happening? Where are the police?* Her phone rang, and she glanced at the caller ID. It was Ellen McCarthy, editor of the *Apple Station Times*.

"Hi, Ellen. Can I call you back?" She glanced toward the trail from the front side, expecting the police to show up at any second.

"Olivia, I need a favor. Get yourself over to Lake Crystal. We have a floater."

She peered toward the dock. "And by floater, you mean?"

"Dead body. Cooper picked up the dispatch call on his scanner app."

"Why is he listening to a police scanner?"

"I have him do it every day to fish for story leads. How do you think we found out about the escaped llamas from Yama's Farm that were terrorizing the soccer fields at the elementary school?"

"Terrorizing is strong language, Ellen. They were eating the grass. That's kind of their thing." She spotted Cole Lee and Bert Branch, two deputies she knew well, along with a female officer she assumed was Jayden Stone. "I'm at the lake right now. I'm the one who called the police about the body."

"Fantastic! How lucky is that? I mean, not for the deceased, of course. Gather whatever information you can. We still should have time to get something on the front page of tomorrow's paper. I'm sending Cooper. Hold on … Cooper, grab your camera. Go to the lake and meet Olivia … Okay, I'm back. Now, Olivia, tell me what you know."

"Whoa, Ellen, wait. Gather information? No. I'm not getting involved in this."

"You already are. I have nobody else here in the office right now. We're short-staffed with Cassandra on vacation."

"You don't have me in the office because I don't work for your paper. I voluntarily write a column occasionally for you in exchange for lunch."

"Olivia, I realize this isn't your thing. All I'm asking is for you to get some quotes, throw together a couple of paragraphs for tomorrow's special edition. Give me something I can use. This is big. Nothing like this has happened since, well, you know."

"No, Ellen. Send someone else. I've gotta go. The police are here."

"There is no one else, and you're already there. You're the star witness. This is a no-brainer."

"A witness? We don't even know whether this is a crime or an accident. It looks like a drowning."

"See, already thinking like an investigative reporter."

"No, I'm not doing—"

"You'll be great! Bring me a story, Olivia!"

The three deputies waved her over as she sighed. "Please, don't send Cooper."

CHAPTER 6

Cole and Bert warmly greeted Olivia as Jayden ripped the softball bat out of her hand. Preston had mentioned the new departmental hire to her one morning during the summer when they ran into each other while getting coffee at Jillian's Cafe. Jayden was every bit as confident, polished, and poised as he had portrayed her. She was by the book, regulation to the nth degree.

Olivia led the three deputies to the end of the dock. The VDEQ fieldworker was as she had left him. Peaceful, as if lulled to sleep by the lake's gentle lapping along the shore. Thin, swirled clusters of algae had coalesced and conformed to his body's contours as if tracing a chalk outline for a crime scene.

She related the sequence of events leading to her discovery of the deceased, and then Jayden escorted her off the dock as Cole and Bert remained behind to heave the victim out of the water and search for physical evidence. Once back on the trail, Jayden asked her to recount her story again, slower and in more detail, as she jotted down the facts in her pocket notebook. When the second interview was complete, Jayden instructed her to wait until officially cleared to leave the scene, then escorted her back to the parking lot. As they emerged from the trail, they met Preston and Chief Payne heading toward them.

"Chief, this is Olivia Penn," Jayden said. "She's the one who found the body. I've taken a preliminary statement. Cole and Bert have control of the scene."

Payne stared down at Olivia. "We're acquainted. You have everything she knows?"

"Yes, sir," Jayden said.

He gestured at the bat. "What's that for?"

"It was in her possession when we arrived. I instructed Ms. Penn to remain in her vehicle, but we located her by the dock with this in hand."

"Ms. Penn, I understand you called in reporting a body you found floating in the lake with a head injury," Payne said. "Can you explain to me what you were doing with that bat?"

She glanced at Preston. "I took it with me for protection. I went back to the dock because I was afraid somebody might come across the body before you arrived."

An approaching vehicle sped down the access road, boisterously crunching gravel as it neared. Preston and

Payne turned, and they all watched as a metallic blue VW Golf zoomed into the lot. The four-door compact swung into a parking spot dangerously close to Preston's F-150. Cooper inched his door open, and then eased out, stood, and pulled a Flat Stanley, turning sideways and squeezing through the cramped space between the two vehicles. Then he hotfooted it around the rear bumper, flung open the passenger side door, and grabbed a camera.

"Deputy Stone, when we're done with Ms. Penn, take your car and close off that access road," Payne said.

"Yes, sir."

Cooper dashed toward them, placing his rainbow-striped camera strap around his neck. He slowed as he approached, clipping a DIY "Press Pass" ID to the pocket of his blue button-down Oxford. Then he raised his camera, lining up a portrait of the chief.

"I would suggest you rethink that," Payne said as he placed his hand on the DSLR's telephoto lens and pushed it away. "Stone, call in the night shift, too. I want all hands on deck. Until we know what we're dealing with, nobody gets in except emergency personnel and the medical examiner."

"I saw the victim earlier, around noon, when he was taking pictures out on the dock," Olivia said. "I was here with a friend. He passed us when he was walking back to his truck, and then we saw him talking with the park ranger."

Payne ignored her. "Stone, get these two out of here. Let's go, detective."

He started toward the lake, but Olivia stepped to her side, blocking him. "You need to talk to Jason."

He stopped and loomed over her. He was the sort that could unhinge a door with one shoulder, and he could've easily brushed her aside with a flick of his wrist. "Why would I want to do that, Ms. Penn?"

"He was here earlier today, too. And then when I went back to the dock after I called the station, he was down by the lake with a boy. Mikey Barns."

Payne turned to Preston. "Do you know who she's talking about?"

Preston eyed Olivia. "This Jason you saw. Gruff-looking guy?" She nodded, and he continued. "That would be Jason Rotterdam. He lives in a mobile home right outside the park boundary. When you're on the park's access road, there's that turnoff coming in. You follow that lane about a quarter mile, and there are some houses set back in the woods."

"Mikey is Melissa Barns' son," Jayden added. "She brings him to the library's 'Read with a Cop' first Friday program. She works there on Saturdays."

"This Rotterdam. Does he have a record?" Payne asked.

"I'm not aware of one," Preston replied. "He's had some gaming violations in the past, but beyond that, I don't know."

"He said he would be at Melissa's house," Olivia offered.

"Deputy, go now and run a check on Rotterdam," Payne said.

Jayden turned and took off toward her patrol car.

An ambulance and a nondescript white sedan pulled into the parking lot. "Here's our ME," Payne said. "I'll go with Dana and the transport to the body. Detective, track down Rotterdam. See what he knows and where he's been today. Anything else I need to know, Ms. Penn?" He paused as she shook her head. "Okay. Now you two get out of here." He turned and stepped toward Dana as she gathered her equipment from her trunk.

Olivia caught Cooper's eye and nodded subtly to his camera and then in Payne's direction. Cooper paced backward several feet and photographed the scene.

"Are you okay?" Preston asked.

She checked her clothes and swiped some grime off her pants. "I'm almost dry now. Still cold, though."

"I meant about finding the victim."

"Yeah, there's that. Not exactly how I expected to start the week," she said while massaging her neck to relieve the tension. "'Tis the season. I had just seen him a few hours before he died. I said hello to him. Now he's dead, just like that. It's unnerving. We go about our days unconscious that our lives could end in a snap. I woke up this morning thinking about meeting A.J. for lunch and working in the afternoon. I gave no thought to the reality that this could

49

be my last day." She sighed, staring at the ground for a moment before looking back up and continuing. "What do you know about Jason? He killed a raccoon by the campgrounds and told us he was out hunting squirrels. Who carries a shotgun in a state park, especially in areas where there are normally other people and children?"

"That's not illegal if he has a permit," Preston said.

"So everyone keeps telling me."

"Why don't you go home. If we have any more questions, we'll be in touch. Or if you remember anything else, call me tonight."

She glanced at Cooper, who had snuck back into the parking lot and was using the ambulance as cover to snap a closer shot of Payne and the ME. "I might have some more questions for *you*," she said.

"I'm not following."

"I somehow agreed to get a statement from the police for Ellen about all of this."

He checked his watch. "Why would you do that?"

"For tomorrow's paper."

"You? Since when did you become a reporter for Ellen's paper? I thought your job is in D.C."

"I'm not, and it is."

"Off the record, get out of here before Payne hears that you've deemed yourself a member of the local press corps. On the record, no comment." He turned and walked away, heading for his truck as Payne and Dana strode toward the lake.

Cooper jogged over to Olivia. "I got some great

shots. What's the plan, boss? What do you think happened?"

She watched as Preston reversed his F-150 and drove out of the lot. "There's no plan. He's right. We should get out of here. As to what happened, I have no idea. It's not for me to figure out."

CHAPTER 7

Olivia arrived in town close to five o'clock and parallel parked shop-side, two suites down from Sophia's clinic. She had dialed the heat to eighty and flipped the seat warmers to max for the twenty-minute drive back. She yawned, feeling as if she had stewed in a sauna, but at least her clothes had dried. She slipped on her socks and shoes and then donned her hoodie to cover her soiled shirt.

She crossed the street and cut through the town square. Her plan was to pop into the newspaper's office and relay to Ellen the facts she knew and then gracefully beg off any further involvement, citing a thorough lack of interest and expertise.

The preparations for Friday's Halloween festival were underway. The main event was always a costume parade in which pint-sized ghosts and ghouls marched along a child-friendly trick-or-treating trail within the square.

Parents would watch from the sidelines, sitting on hay bales while snacking on funnel cakes and sipping spiced cider.

It was a far cry from when she was a child. She and A.J. would go trick-or-treating for hours unsupervised. They carried flashlights and pillowcases, executing their schemed route with tactical precision. Full-sized candy bars were the priority. They passed through familiar neighborhoods, eschewing perfectly lit and friendly homes, and watched as the inexperienced trotted along the sidewalks, singsonging "trick-or-treat." Suckers. She and A.J. would slide stealthily by, not distracted by the dull promises of candy corn or licorice. Their prime aim: chocolate. And lots of it. By the evening's end, copious sweet treats would weigh down their pillowcases from their plundering. By the morning, though, their stomachs always rebelled, rumbling and aching with pain and regret.

"Hello, Olivia," Dorothy Peabody said, waving from where she sat on a park bench next to her husband, Floyd. She held a small cup of coffee while he scrolled on his phone. A paper sack from Jillian's Cafe rested between them.

The long-married couple was a fixture in Apple Station. Olivia often would see them strolling arm in arm along the town square when the weather was pleasant. They were the sort that could sit silently, side by side, for an hour or more without speaking, but still know exactly what the other was thinking. Dorothy knew just enough about everyone to be better informed than the average gossip. Floyd had no issues with saying whatever he wanted, whenever he wanted. Except to Dorothy. He was uncensored and practical, but certainly no fool.

Today, they both had dressed for winter, though the temperature was anchored firmly in the fifties. Dorothy sported a fashionable, shiny silver down jacket while Floyd leaned more conservative with a charcoal wool driving coat.

"Hi, Mr. and Mrs. Peabody. Are you enjoying the afternoon?" Olivia said.

Dorothy warmly smiled. "It's a little chilly for us senior folk, but we like to soak up as much sun in the fall as we can. I hate winter. We'll soon be stuck inside until spring arrives." She pondered Olivia for a moment. "You look different today, dear. Are you doing something new with your hair?"

Olivia combed her fingers through the lengths of her hair, examining the ends. Several inches had gotten wet from her lake dip and had air-dried, leaving behind a frizzy mess. She pulled out a scrunchy from her pocket and fashioned a ponytail.

Dorothy grabbed the bag from Jillian's sitting next to her on the bench and held it out toward Olivia. "I'm sorry. I'm being rude. Would you like an oatmeal raisin cookie?"

She wanted a steaming hot shower. She wanted to sanitize, maybe torch, her grimy, smelly clothes. She wanted to rewind the day, start over, and make sure Buddy had his stupid red ball with him before leaving the park with A.J. With none of these possible in the moment, though, the best option appeared to be a cookie.

"Yes, please." She plucked one of the oversized treats from the bag and chomped off a comforting chunk as if it were a loaf of rustic sourdough bread.

"They have chocolate chips in them, too," Floyd said. He turned his phone's screen toward Olivia. "I can read on this thing."

Dorothy held her hands up in mock surprise. "Let's stop the presses."

Floyd continued, either ignoring or not even hearing her. With him, it was hard to tell. "Look here. This is the mystery I'm reading now. I hit this icon, and then I can access all my e-books in my e-library."

Dorothy snickered. "Olivia, do you have an E-I-E-I-O library on your phone, too?"

Olivia bit back a smile and leaned in closer to Floyd. Not too close, though, as she feared she reeked of Lake Crystal. "That's amazing, Mr. Peabody. Have you given up your paperbacks?"

He focused on his screen and grumbled under his breath. "The wife says I have too many."

"You could donate the ones you no longer want, or leave them in the little library," Olivia said. "Then you'd have room for new books on your shelves."

He pointed across the square to a vacant suite close

by Sophia's clinic. "Is that what's going in that empty store? That'll be convenient."

She turned and gestured toward the lawn's opposite end. "No. Can you see that large box on the post down there? Right between the gazebo and playground?"

"The big birdhouse?" he asked.

She laughed. "That's a little library. You can leave books there, and anyone can come by and take them."

"You don't say." He turned toward Dorothy. "Did you know about this?" He scooted to the edge of the bench, as if the few extra inches afforded him a better view. He watched as a woman opened the quaint, farmhouse-themed box, and then donated several books from her backpack before choosing one for herself to take home. "Why, I'll be. You say it's free?"

Dorothy stared at Olivia, raising her eyebrows while subtly shaking her head. Olivia understood. Ixnay the topic. She bit off another sizable chunk of her cookie, craving a glass of cold milk. "These are fantastic cookies."

"The days are getting chilly," Dorothy said. She tapped Floyd on the arm. "Zip up your jacket. I don't want you getting sick."

Dutifully, he did as he was told. He patted her hand. "She's always looking out for me. That's why I keep her around." They both laughed as Dorothy playfully slapped his knee.

"I like your coat, Mrs. Peabody."

Floyd poked at one of the quilted silvery sections of the puffer coat. "She looks like she's going to the moon."

Dorothy dismissed the style critique, waving her hand as if shooing away a gnat. "I bought it online with a coupon code. I'm as snug as a bug in a rug. Thank you very much."

"I told her she could wear it for the costume parade and go dressed as the tin man."

"And you'd make a fine scarecrow with your chicken legs," Dorothy countered.

Floyd chuckled and clucked, and then hiked up his pants, revealing his skinny lower legs.

"Are you two coming to watch the parade?" Olivia asked.

Dorothy nodded. "We're the honorary grand marshals. We don't do any high stepping or baton twirling, but we get to wear sashes and pass out treats at the end of the trail."

Floyd tapped Dorothy on her arm. "Did you see that? Somebody just took two books. What happens if the library runs out?"

He reached for another cookie, but Dorothy snatched the paper sack away. "That's enough for you." She looked back at Olivia. "Last year, we dressed up as Fred Astaire and Ginger Rogers."

"That's so sweet." She had little doubt who would take the lead between the two of them.

Floyd straightened, placing his hands on his knees. "Every man should know how to dance. Before you marry anyone, make sure he knows how to spin you around the ballroom."

"That's the best advice I've heard all day, Mr. Peabody. I'll add that to my checklist."

Dorothy prodded his elbow. "That reminds me. Rose told me while she was doing my hair this week that the library is screening *Swing Time* for the next senior cinema Saturday." She looked up at Olivia. "The second Saturday of each month, they show movies at the library. They're free for seniors. Five dollars for everyone else. You should bring your father. Get there early, though, if you want a good seat."

"How do they show movies there?"

"In the conference room," Dorothy replied. "They have big, comfy chairs. The kind that swivel and rock. There are three levels of seating, and the screen's up front. There's a nice young woman who helps to get everyone settled. She always saves us seats down in front, so we don't have to walk up the steps. She brings her son with her, and he watches all the golden oldies with us. Doesn't say a word, he just sits there."

"Are you talking about Melissa, by any chance?" Olivia asked.

"Yes, that's right. Do you know her?"

"Not exactly. I know she lives out by the lake."

Floyd rocked on the edge of the bench three times and then stood slowly over a count of five. "Near to that prepper. You about ready to go, dear? That coffee's run right through me."

Dorothy folded over the cookie bag's top and then stashed it inside her purse. She stacked the two empty paper cups, stood, and threw them in a mesh bin behind the bench. "Please excuse us, Olivia. Nature is calling."

"Mr. Peabody, who are you talking about?"

"The prepper? What's his name, Dorothy? He always looks like he's going hunting."

"Jason," Dorothy said. "Don't listen to him, Olivia. Melissa tells me he watches Mikey sometimes. It's got to be hard for her, living by herself. That boy of hers keeps her busy."

"You're right, dear. Jason's his name. He's a strange one. Remember, we saw him last week at the garden center? We were buying mums for her box planters, and he was there loading up his truck. The entire bed was full of fertilizer and soil."

Dorothy interlocked her arm with his. "You got me there, sweetie. That qualifies him as strange. It seems more like he's planting something. Not planning for the end of the world."

He rested his hand on top of hers. "You laugh now, but someday, you'll see."

"Come on, handsome. Let's get you home before Olivia thinks you've lost your marbles. Goodbye, dear."

Olivia returned the parting pleasantries and then crossed the street. She had to admit Jason had a certain creep factor about him, which was only reinforced by what Floyd had said. Still, none of this involved her. After all, she had a survival field manual in her library.

She wasn't planning to stock up on emergency rations, but she had bought a hand-crank analog radio with a built-in flashlight in case of an electromagnetic pulse.

She opened the door to the newspaper's suite and stepped inside. "Hey, Cooper."

Ellen bustled out of her office and snapped her fingers twice. "Olivia, come here." She grabbed Olivia's elbow and positioned her two feet from the whiteboard on the back wall. Then she lifted Cooper's camera from his desk and lined up a shot.

"What's happening here, Ellen?"

She lowered the DSLR, scanning Olivia from head to toe. "Is this a new look for you?"

She straightened the hemline of her hoodie and zipped it to the top. "I haven't changed clothes since my dip in the lake."

"I want to get a picture of you to include with tomorrow's headline: 'Key Witness Recounts Horrifying Scene at Lake Crystal.' Or something like that. I'll fiddle with the exacts later."

Olivia stepped away from the whiteboard and sat at Paige's former desk. "I'll write up what I know—what I can say that doesn't interfere with the police investigation. Which isn't much. But no more. Chances are that the police won't know anything for a few days. By then, Cassandra will be back."

Ellen set the camera on top of a file cabinet. "Do you have a high-resolution head shot I can use for the front page? And it's got to be you. You have access that nobody else has, with your special arrangement."

Olivia leaned forward, pinning her elbows on the desk. "My what?"

"Your inside connection with the detective. Bev's son."

She shook her head. "No. I don't have any connection with him. Who told you that?"

Ellen turned toward Cooper, who was working at his desk. He glanced at Olivia and then hid his face behind his laptop's screen.

Olivia eyed Cooper, speaking as if to the rear of an ample auditorium. "Your information is wrong."

He peeked up and then dipped his head again.

Ellen's office phone rang. "That's me. Get me that story ASAP."

Olivia leaned back in her chair, remembering the spark in Paige's eyes whenever she scoped out a hot lead on a juicy story. Paige somehow would have spun finding a dead person at Lake Crystal into a grand conspiracy. Maybe even a mob hit. The Mafia would definitely be involved. An organized crime syndicate in Apple Station. The headline: "Goodfellas Don't Make Good Neighbors." Yes, this had Paige written all over it. *You're probably jealous right now that it's me instead of you who found the body. I wish it had been you.*

Though she couldn't muster Paige's certain enthusiasm for deep diving into the details surrounding the fieldworker's death, she could at least be professional and provide Ellen with a factual piece she could run. It's what Paige would have done. It's what she would do. She flipped open the laptop on the desk, drafting the opening paragraph in her head as the system booted.

When she had worked for a mid-Atlantic publisher of local presses after graduate school, she had covered everything: town politics, bake sales, homecoming games. Her beat was simply "the news." But it had been a while since she had written a news article unrelated to her advice column.

She stared at the white screen for several minutes, and then wrote and rewrote the first sentence five times. She closed the program and then reopened it, as if all she needed was a nod from her muse and a new blank page.

"So, what are you going to write?" Cooper asked.

She glanced up as he leaned with both hands on her desk, inching uncomfortably close into her personal space. "Just the facts. We can't speculate. It was probably an accident."

"Is that what you really think happened?"

She scooted back and folded her arms. "I don't know. I still can't believe that just a few hours ago I said hi to him, and now he's dead. The whole thing seems suspicious, but I can't write that without evidence. You should jot down everything you remember about the scene and give the notes to Cassandra when she returns."

"Right-o, chief. I'm on it." He pivoted and hurriedly stepped to his desk.

Olivia slid the laptop closer, cracked her knuckles,

and got back to it. After ten minutes of mentally hemming and hawing, she hit her stride and typed the last period on her piece. She emailed the document to Ellen, shut down the laptop, and prepared to leave.

"I'm out of here, Cooper. See you when I see you."

"Is this it?" Ellen yelled from inside her office.

Olivia peeked over her shoulder as she beelined for the door.

"I think she's talking to you," Cooper said.

Ellen burst out into the workroom waving a single sheet of paper, turning it front to back. "There's so much white space here, I could use this to surrender."

Olivia turned halfway. "That's all I know."

Ellen glanced at her watch. "Okay. Go. I'll value add to it if we learn anything over the next two hours. I'm firing off a press release: 'Famed Advice Columnist Investigates Hometown Murder.' That's going to get eyeballs. Cooper, post that across all the socials."

Olivia backed out of the door to the cheerful jingling from a cluster of bells hanging from the handle. "Please, Ellen. Don't do that. Leave me out of everything."

CHAPTER 8

Olivia crossed the street, planning a pit stop at Sophia's clinic to excuse herself from dinner. Though she was crashing from her cookie sugar high and a warm, home-made meal sounded tempting, patches of skin on her arms and hands were alarmingly red and itchy. She would opt to sacrifice supper for a shower and settle for cereal at home, if her dad already had finished last night's leftovers.

Sophia's clinic was once a bakery that had been the local go-to for sweet treats for all occasions. When the former owners retired, Sophia leased the suite along Blossom Avenue and hired A.J. to redesign and convert the interior to suit her practice needs. He had downsized the commercial kitchen, leaving intact select appliances while reconfiguring the space to accommodate a modest dining area. Now, about once a week, after Sophia was done with her sessions for the day, her grandmother would prepare an elaborate, traditional Mexican feast for friends and family.

Olivia's stomach rumbled as she strolled across the town lawn. Dusk had settled over the sunset, shading the sky with ombres of violet and blue. Black iron post lamps lining the streets flickered and then shone bright, ready to illuminate the sidewalks with soft, golden light.

Two young boys frolicked, seizing the last play from the day, as their mothers chatted on a nearby bench. The taller of the two dropped back and hurled a football a mile over his friend's outstretched hands. The ball tumbled end over end and came to a stop at Olivia's feet. She grabbed the football and spun it, without looking, until her pinky and ring finger lay across the laces. Hours of backyard toss with her father when she was a child had ingrained the proper grip and mechanics. She reeled back, stepped forward, and fired a spiral straight to her target.

"She throws better than you, and she's a girl," the taller boy said.

His friend tackled him and playfully punched his ribs. "If you like her so much, why don't you marry her?"

She laughed to herself as she crossed the street, musing that she may have to adopt a new strategy in game planning the affairs of her heart. As she entered the clinic, the seductive smell of slow-cooked pork wooed her immediately.

"Is that you, Liv?" Sophia yelled from inside the play gym.

Tori emerged from the treatment room and sauntered into the foyer, carrying her son Tyler on her hip. "Yeah, it's her, the one and only," Tori said with a playful smile.

She set Tyler on the ground, and he quickly crawled over to Olivia. He came up tall on his knees, grabbed her pants, and pulled himself into standing.

"Look at you, Tyler. Such a big, strong boy," Olivia said.

Tori smoothed his rumpled hair. "That's his new trick. He finds it quite entertaining to pull this hocus-pocus at the coffee table. You like to grab everything in reach and try to make it disappear, don't you, my little pumpkin?"

He giggled and let go of Olivia's pants, dropping on his rear.

"Just you wait until you have your own bundle of joy. If you ever want practice, you can take this one any time. Mamma is long overdue for a spa day."

Tyler pulled at and loosened Olivia's shoelaces. "As an honorary auntie, I'm always happy to babysit this cutie," she said.

"From your lips to God's ear. You said it. No backsies. I'm booking a massage and manicure for next week." Tori swooped Tyler off the floor. "We've got to get on our way. Ty needs a bath, and I need a glass of pinot noir. We expect to see you on Friday for the parade."

Olivia exchanged a high five with Tyler. "Wouldn't miss it."

Sophia strode into the foyer as Tori was leaving. "I think dinner is almost ready," she said.

"It smells great, but I can't stay."

"What's up? Why not?"

Olivia bent over to tie her shoelaces and then stood tall, peeking down the hallway that connected the foyer to the back of the building. "Are your mother and grand-mother in the kitchen?"

"Yes. My dad is working the night shift in the ER. It's just us tonight."

Olivia sidled over to the children's play corner, waving for Sophia to follow. She discreetly detailed her two trips to Lake Crystal, and then plopped down in a heap on the sofa. "So, you can see why I want to go home, clean up, and change."

Sophia glanced down the hallway and then sat on the sofa next to her, keeping her voice low. "I get it. I can't imagine going through that. I can't believe someone died at the lake. I go there all the time. You should've called me earlier. Why didn't you? Are the police treating this as a murder? You were there by your-self. If somebody killed that guy, he still could've been there."

Olivia leaned back into the sofa's cozy cushions. "I don't know. The police were just starting the investigation when I left. I'm sure it's too soon to tell. I didn't call earlier because I knew I was coming here, and I haven't had time. I went straight to the newspaper's office after I left the park."

"Are you now covering this story for the paper? What about Cassandra—isn't this kind of her thing?"

"She's out of town, and no, I'm not covering this for the paper. Today was just a favor for Ellen, really. A one and done. I told the police what I knew and wrote a brief piece for her. That's it."

"Let's hope so. Are you sure you're okay? To say you've had an awful day is underselling it."

"It wasn't the Monday I had planned. But whoever that guy was from the VDEQ, he got the short end of the stick."

Josefina shuffled from the hallway into the foyer. "We're ready to eat."

"Abuela, Liv can't stay. She needs to get home."

"Is it your father? Is he okay?"

"Yes, he's fine," Olivia replied. "It's just that—"

"Then you stay," Josefina said with a matriarchal air. She lit up with a smile Olivia couldn't contest and walked back through the hallway to the kitchen.

"If you want to go, I'll tell them you weren't feeling well," Sophia said. "Or if you want to hang out for a while, and feel like putting something fresh on, I have a shirt you can change into."

Olivia grimaced as a wave of nausea hit. "Truthfully, I'm starving, and supper smells wonderful. I think my blood sugar is tanking. If you don't mind me borrowing a shirt, I would love to stay."

Sophia strode to the hallway and opened a supply closet opposite the treatment room. Then she returned and unfurled a T-shirt, displaying the custom design graphic: "PTs: We keep you moving and grooving."

Olivia stood and accepted the shirt. "That's cute. Give me a few minutes to clean up, and then I'll be right in." She ducked into the bathroom in the hallway and changed shirts, washed her face, and scrubbed her arms and hands. A few quality minutes with soap and water made her feel halfway human and presentable. She bundled her hoodie and shirt together, leaving them on the couch in the foyer, and then she joined Sophia's family in the kitchen.

"Mija, good to see you," Maria, Sophia's mother, said. She hugged Olivia and then kept an arm wrapped around her shoulders as she pondered the borrowed T-shirt. "Are you taking up a new profession?"

"No, it's just on loan for the evening."

Maria released her and slid a chair away from the rustic, sunglow linen-covered table. "I'm sure there's a story behind that. Come sit down."

Josefina lifted a hefty platter of pork from atop the six-burner stove, and Sophia quickstepped around her chair to take the heavy load from her and set it on the table.

"Abuela, sit. I'll get the rest." Sophia placed family-sized serving bowls of black beans and rice and apple pecan salad next to the platter.

Olivia's gaze went from the enticing meal to the

counter under the cabinets, lined end to end with trays of tempting sweet treats.

"Mamá has been baking for the library fundraiser for Friday's festival," Maria said.

Olivia fixated on a bread board brimming with pan de muerto, mesmerized by the comforting allure of calming carbs. "I hope I don't have to wait until then to sample some, or all, of that. Are you selling the sugar skulls too?"

"Sí. Las Calaveras. Those are for our Día de los Muertos celebration on Saturday, but Mamá is taking some for the bake sale. They sell out quickly." Every year, Sophia's family honored their deceased ancestors with a traditional Day of the Dead celebration over the first two days of November. "Will you be able to join us at our home?"

"Of course."

"Sophia suggested we go as a family to the cemetery to remember Paige as well," Maria said. "Her mother is meeting us there."

"That's a great idea, Soph. That'll mean a lot to June."

Josefina made the sign of the cross, signifying that all could dig in and pass the food around the table. Olivia loaded up with a healthy helping of apple salad and pork, while Josefina liberally scooped rice and beans onto her plate for her.

Maria placed her napkin on her lap. "How's your wrist been?"

Olivia flexed her fingers, forming a fist. "All healed. Soph worked her magic, sometimes disguised as pain."

"You're most welcome, bestie."

"What about your father? Is he well?" Maria asked.

"Yes. He keeps himself busy. He's been exercising more by walking with Buddy, which has been good for both of them."

Maria spooned rice onto her own plate. "Have you thought anymore about your long-term plans? Do you think you'll be staying here, or do you want to move back to D.C.?"

Olivia slowly chewed a forkful of pulled pork, unsure of how to answer the question she asked herself daily. She had straddled both lives comfortably for the months that she had been back home, keeping a foot firmly in each. At some point, though, the parallel lives would diverge too far, and she would have to choose. She didn't want to leave her father, but she knew he wouldn't want her to stay for his sake. The longer she was away from her former life, the harder it would be to resume—if that's what she even wanted.

"You should stay here, take care of your father," Josefina said.

"Ay, Mamá," Maria countered.

"I don't think my dad needs to be taken care of. As for me, I'm not sure. We'll see what happens."

"Sí, mija. Time will tell. The only thing for sure is that nothing is certain. Life is about change."

Olivia breathed in Maria's words, allowing them to

settle for a moment, and then looked back at the counter. "Is all of that being donated for the library sale?"

"That's just the test baking," Sophia said. "You know Abuela, everything must be the best. And it always is."

"We could use some more help on the planning committee, if you have any free time," Maria said. "I'm surprised Ellen hasn't brought it up to you. We're meeting tomorrow at the inn if you want to join us. I'm sure Bev would love to see you there." Apple Station Inn was a popular meeting place for community groups, and as the owner, Bev Styles always made them welcome.

Sophia glanced at Olivia and said, "Melissa will be there."

Maria nodded. "Sí. She told me she's thinking of restarting PT for Mikey."

"You've seen him for therapy?" Olivia asked.

Sophia shook her head at her mother. "Privacy? HIPPA? Anyone?"

Maria set her fork on her plate. "He's on the autism spectrum. Sophia worked with him for a few months last year."

"Mamá, you can't just announce that to the world."

"No, mija. It's you who can't. I can say what I want. Besides, everyone who knows her knows that. And the world isn't here with us tonight." She winked at Olivia. "Is Melissa a friend of yours?"

"Not really. I met Mikey briefly today by the lake." She left it at that, not wanting to rehash her day, and then changed the subject. "Tell me more about the fundraiser."

Maria readily related the ins and outs of the sale as they continued with dinner. At the end of the meal, Maria packed up leftovers and a week's worth of baked treats for Olivia to take home to share with her father. After they said their goodbyes, Sophia accompanied her out into the foyer.

Olivia grabbed her dirty, bundled clothes off the couch. "I'll get your shirt back to you tomorrow."

Sophia waved her hand, dismissing any urgency. "Please, I've got plenty. Besides, I know where you live. Thanks for staying a while. You know how much these dinners mean to my grandmother. Call me if you have any trouble sleeping tonight. No matter the time."

It was after eight when she left the clinic. Gray clouds now streaked the night sky, obscuring the stars and granting only glimpses of the full, luminous moon. She unlocked her car, got in, and placed Maria's tote bag of leftovers and desserts on the passenger seat.

A handful of revelers huddled around the community fire pit, warming themselves and conversing loudly. The scene replayed every fall and winter from October to December. A local masonry contractor always ensconced the temporary stone-enclosed steel pit near the gazebo, and it blazed from six to nine each evening. For as long as she could remember, volunteers from the civic association stoked the fire with apple wood supplied by an orchard in Bluemont. She had spent many evenings there on visits home with her friends, watching the flickering flames, making s'mores, and reminiscing. Now, with older eyes, though it looked the same, the scene seemed different. She recalled what Maria had said about the only certainty in life being change, and then she thought ahead to a year from now, unable to imagine where she may be.

CHAPTER 9

Olivia eased into Tuesday morning, warmly wrapped by a quilted down duvet. She rolled to her side, reluctant to open her groggy eyes to welcome the day. Last night, she had arrived back home to find her father sleeping on the sofa with *A Quiet Place* streaming on the TV. There had been no need to wake him. Instead, she had lingered for half an hour in a steamy shower until her shoulders softened and her toes wrinkled. Afterwards, she couldn't fall asleep. She had cycled through all her go-tos: reading, checking e-mail, and listening to binaural beats. Nothing had worked, though, until she drifted off to a piano lullaby sometime after three.

Soft whining emanated near the foot of her bed, and she peeked over the side, spying Buddy's wide eyes and white-tipped tail gently swaying. "How'd you get in here?" She always left her door cracked at night, and this morning it stood nudged half open. Her cell's screen showed a quarter past eight. "Sorry, Buddy. I'm not awake yet. Try again in an hour."

He placed his forepaws on the box spring and bit twice into his squeaky bone. She grunted and reached down, wrestling the annoying toy from him.

"Why do you still have this?" She flipped it through the opened door.

He bolted after the bone and returned before she could finish fluffing her pillow for a planned five-minute snooze. She flung her covers off and sprung up as he barked, anticipating a spirited game of fetch.

"Mission accomplished, little rascal. You got me up. Let's go." She puttered out of her bedroom, through the hallway, and to the top of the staircase. She tossed the toy down the steps, and Buddy scampered after it. "Now stay down there. Play with Dad until I change."

She returned to her room, made her bed, and righted a small teddy bear dressed as a Texas Ranger on her nightstand. The plush cub had been a get-well gift from Preston's mother. As she unplugged her phone from its charging cord, the screen lit, displaying two missed texts. She reflexively opened the first message a split second before registering the contact associated with the number.

She read: "I just heard what happened to you in May. I'm sorry, I didn't know. Are you okay? Why didn't you call me? I would've come. I'm sorry I wasn't there for you. Can we talk?" She perched on the edge of the bed, blindsided as her heart ramped up its rhythm. The second message, directly underneath, added: "Miss you. Miss us."

She stared at the screen and then slammed the cell into her pillow, feeling her pulse pump in her throat. Daniel. Six months and no word until now. A two-year relationship primed for marriage had unraveled over four weeks. They had let it happen, and she long ago stopped wondering why. She shot up and yanked open her dresser drawer, snatching a shirt and pair of socks.

This wasn't how she wanted to start the day. She banged the drawer shut and then sharply tugged the mini-blind cord, letting in the morning light. Her throat tightened, and her grip choked the life out of her clothes. *Unbelievable. You text me after midnight on a random Tuesday, after all this time.*

There had been no ultimatums between them or a last resort knock-down fight. Though their parting was mutual, encouraged by evolving careers on opposite coasts, it wasn't without a niggling doubt about what could've been. In six months, they hadn't even spoken. She harbored no ill-will, and she wished him well, but still. The thought of calling had crossed her mind many times, but why, and what would she say?

She blew out a full breath of steam and reread the second message: "Miss you. Miss us." It had been months since she had considered him anything other than a part of her past. His words, though, flowed along a familiar current in her heart. She started a reply that soon stretched the screen's full length, but then thought twice and let her feelings rest unsent. She got dressed and took her phone with her downstairs.

Buddy welcomed her at the bottom of the steps and followed her into the kitchen. Her father was sitting at the table with a stoneware mug on a napkin and the newspaper spread out in front of him.

"Good morning, Dad. Did you eat anything yet?"

He closed the newspaper's front section and then folded it in half. "Lost my appetite."

She reached into the cabinet for a coffee cup. "Are you feeling alright?"

"We got a special edition of the *Apple Station Times* today. You wanna hear the lead headline?"

She dripped coffee into her cup from the glass carafe, keeping her back turned. "Aha."

"Body found at Lake Crystal. Local reporter investigates cover-up."

She spun, eyeing her head shot from her press page and a photo of her and Preston from yesterday aligned side by side under the headline. "What?"

"Wait, it gets better. Famed hometown columnist, Olivia Penn, investigating. Suspects foul play."

She grabbed the front section, scanned to the byline, and clenched her teeth. "Cooper." She slapped the newspaper headline down onto the table.

Her father flipped the paper over, removed his glasses, and placed them on her photo. "Would you care to explain to me what this is about?"

She sat beside him, took a slow, measured sip of

coffee, and then centered a crystal bowl of Jack Be Little mini pumpkins from their summer garden. "You were sleeping last night when I got back, and I didn't want to wake you."

He tapped the headline. "No, this. Explain this."

She related the facts as she knew them, stressing the article had blown her implied involvement out of proportion. She left out most of the worrisome details and doubled down on the spin that she hadn't been in any danger.

He was silent as she told her tale, and then he lectured her for ten minutes, expressing his deep-seated relief and concern. When he had finished, he asked for her word. "Don't get involved in this. You understand?"

"I'm not. I'm just—"

"Don't say it. I don't even want to hear it."

"Dad, let me finish. I helped Ellen out yesterday. This normally would be Cassandra's beat, but she's away. Need I remind you that this is your fault, anyway? You're the one who insisted I go back to look for Buddy's ball. Now, I'm involved. I found the body."

"I didn't ask you to find a body. I asked you to find Buddy's ball. Your only involvement should be with the police. You don't work for Ellen. Your job is in D.C. Not here. It's not on you to cover this, even if you're just doing Ellen a favor."

"I'm not covering it. That's not what I'm doing. Ellen's short-staffed right now. This is the sort of story Paige would've been giddy to investigate. But not me. If anything, I'll get the standard no comment runaround by the police, and that will be that. They'll probably not even know anything for days, anyway. I write for a living. That's what I do. Before I started the advice column, I wrote all kinds of stories. I think I can manage a few paragraphs."

Buddy hopped out of his dog bed, meandered over, and lay by her feet. She bent forward, patted his side, and scratched behind his ears.

Her father stood and washed his mug in the sink. "You never covered a murder you were involved with. Isn't there some sort of conflict of interest there? If not, there should be."

"That's not really a thing in this case."

"Please, honey, do only what you need to do and nothing more."

She rose, reassuring him with a side hug. "I promise."

He swiped his keys and phone from the counter and then removed a leash from the hook rack. "It's time to take Buddy for his walk. He gets grouchy if I don't."

She grabbed a vanilla yogurt and half pint of blueberries from the refrigerator. "Funny, he says the same thing about you."

He clipped the leash to Buddy's collar. "Are you sure you have to go to the police station? Can't you just call Preston and get your official statement that way?"

She shook her head without hesitating. "No. I can't call him." She sat back at the table, swiveled in her seat, and pulled out a spoon from the drawer. "I'm thinking of speaking with Kevin Fields instead. He's a park ranger I met yesterday. His parents own Fields Farm out on the Snickersville Turnpike. A.J. knows his brother. Kevin is on the periphery of all this. I thought some quotes from him would satisfy Ellen since I'm sure I would get absolutely nothing from the police. I'd like to avoid going to the police station if I can."

He opened the kitchen door. "That sounds like a plan. Stay out of trouble. Let's go, Buddy. It's time for you to take me for a walk."

She perused the article in the paper while eating and then jotted down a few questions for Kevin in a note-taking app on her phone. The text she had drafted to Daniel stood open like a sore thumb. She scanned what she had written with a cooler head and backspaced over it all.

CHAPTER 10

After breakfast, Olivia chanced a trip to the lake, gambling that Kevin would have a stepped-up presence in patrolling the park in the aftermath of yesterday's discovery. She pulled into the lot at ten o'clock, joining three other cars already there. Kevin's SUV wasn't among them. She parked next to a police cruiser, guessing that either Cole or Burt was investigating lakeside by the dock.

She got out and locked up, planning to pepper whatever authority she could find with questions. A young woman and someone Olivia suspected was her mother sat at a picnic table in a pavilion near a silver crossover hybrid.

A spirited girl of preschool age charged toward Olivia, hollering and waving a stick. "Stop! You're my prisoner now!"

She smiled at the child, musing that the butterfly

patches on the knees of her jeans belied the cutie's fierceness. She held her hands up. "I surrender."

"Ava, leave her alone!" the younger woman said. "Get back over here. Sorry, miss!"

The youngster stood her ground, holding her stick up high. Olivia waved over to the two women. "It's okay," she said while squatting. "Ava, will you please let me go? I promise I won't ever, ever, ever come into your kingdom again without asking you first."

Ava giggled and grinned, revealing a pair of missing front teeth. She spun and skipped away, slashing her stick and saving her imaginary friends from her make-believe dragons.

Olivia hiked along the trail leading to the lake. The trees stood sparser than yesterday as more leaves had fallen overnight. When she reached the clearing and was within view of the lake, she recognized Bert's lanky silhouette on the dock. Her sight shifted to a couple strolling hand in hand toward her. The man looked like a cover model for a high-end apparel brand, in khakis and a navy plaid button-down shirt. The woman was at least six inches shorter and functionally dressed for field work. She wore hiking boots, a rain jacket, and pants with enough pockets to stash anything needed for survival in the wilderness.

Olivia politely smiled. "Hi."

"Good morning," the man said. "If you're heading for the dock, the police are investigating an incident that happened here yesterday. I don't think they want anyone out there right now."

She eyed Bert. "Unfortunately, I'm personally aware of the incident."

"I'm sorry," he said. "Was it … someone you knew?"

"No. I'm the one who found the body."

The woman gasped. "Oh, wow. That must've been horrible."

"You're that reporter from the paper," he said. "I thought you looked familiar. I saw your picture this morning. Olivia Penn, right? I read the article. You think this was a suspicious death? Have you come to grill the police?"

"No. I mean, I'm not sure. I didn't come to interview the police. I didn't even know they'd be here. I'm trying to find a park ranger I spoke with yesterday. Kevin Fields."

He looked at the woman and released her hand. "I haven't seen him today. I should introduce us. I'm Chris, his brother. This is Dr. Jennifer Lovelace. Otherwise known as my bride-to-be."

His fiancée rolled her eyes like an embarrassed teen. She extended her hand toward Olivia, and they shook. "Jenn is fine."

"Kevin mentioned something about a wedding yesterday. So that's you two. That's wonderful. Congratulations. You're a doctor?"

"I have a PhD in agricultural and bio systems engineering. I specialize in natural resource engineering for utilization and conservation of soil and water."

"That's both impressive and a mouthful," Olivia said.

Jenn gave a wide smile that popped the apples of her cheeks. "Sorry. Sometimes I forget to take off my science hat. I'm not that nerdy all the time."

"I would like to counter that," Chris said.

Jenn turned slightly toward him. "And I will counter your counter. Some of us don't want to be sitting behind a computer screen all day when we could be outside, enjoying the fresh air and sunshine." She looked back at Olivia and then over her shoulder. "I wanted to see the algae bloom for myself."

Chris wrapped an arm around her waist. "She's the only person I know who thinks a bunch of green goo is fascinating."

"A.J. and I saw it yesterday," Olivia said. "He said it's not unusual for blooms to occur around here."

"A.J., oh gosh," Chis said. "I haven't spoken with him for such a long time. Kevin didn't mention seeing him yesterday. How's he been?"

"He's doing well. He leased out a vacant suite in town and set up shop as a general contractor."

"Good for him. We have a few things that need sprucing up around the farm before we sell. I'll have to call him and see if he has time to do some work for us."

"Your friend, A.J., is right about the blooms," Jenn said. "They develop for a variety of reasons. Overabundance of nutrients, high temperatures, water stagnation.

The state may decide to shut down the park until it clears. The toxins produced can be hazardous to the entire ecosystem. I wouldn't go swimming in the lake right now if I were you."

Olivia itched the back of her hand. "Yeah, that seems ill-advised."

"I hate to see the bloom get out of hand," Jenn continued. "The birds, fish, everything in the water is at risk."

Chris removed his arm from her waist and slipped his fingertips into his pockets. "We know who's responsible for it."

Jenn turned toward him. "We don't know that at all."

"Well, I do. We almost lost our organic certification because of him last year."

"Who are you talking about?" Olivia asked.

"Philip Wayne. He owns Whispering Meadows Country Club. The eastern edge of his property is adjacent to our back fields. Both of our properties border the parkland's north boundary. His golf course and everything on that property always look healthy, even when the area is experiencing a drought. He has to be dumping massive amounts of chemicals to keep the grounds looking like that year-round. My parents had to jump through all kinds of testing hoops last October to prove we were following USDA organic standards when the EPA tested soil samples from his golf course and found high levels of contaminants. He accused us of polluting

his land. Can you believe that? We're an organic operation, and he accused us."

Jenn intertwined her arm with his. "Easy now, Chris.
That's in the past, and what's going on here with the
bloom is something that happens naturally all the time."

Chris bent down and kissed her cheek. "She keeps
me in line. She won't toot her own horn, but she's a
champion for environmental conservation. That's why I
asked, more like begged, her to come on board three
years ago when my parents converted their farm to an
organic operation. It's better for the land, more profitable
for us, and provides a higher quality product for the
consumer. Jenn did such a great job, and I couldn't bear
to let her go, so I asked her to marry me."

Jenn leaned her head against his shoulder. "It turned
out to be the best job ever."

Olivia half-smiled, feeling as if she had been
ambushed by a vat of sap. She bit the bullet and asked,
"When's the wedding?"

They gazed at each other like lovesick puppies. "In a
couple of months," Jenn said as Chris held up two fingers
for emphasis.

"You must be crazy busy between planning for that
and the sale of the farm. You're not interested in keeping
the farm in the family? You two seem like a perfect fit to
take over the operation."

Chris shook his head. "Maybe a fit for life, but not a
fit to be business partners. I'm a numbers guy. Agricultural system manager by trade. I analyze the data to

strategize how to increase crop yields while minimizing costs."

"While protecting the environment," Jenn added.

"Yes, of course. While protecting the environment. I'm not a hands-in-the-dirt farmer like my dad. I've been trying to get him to retire for years now. He's up at four o'clock every morning, and then he works all day until my mom calls him in for dinner. Both his knees are bad, but he refuses to slow down. As long as the farm is in the family, he'd still be out there working every day. He only agreed to sell when I told him how hard it was for my mom to manage the place. They're both in their seventies, and they deserve to sit back and relax, enjoy their life without the pressure of dealing with the daily operations of a farm as big as theirs. It's nonstop, stressful work."

"It's nice your family is so close," Olivia said. "Is Kevin involved in the business at all?"

"He was for a while, but it got to be a bit much for him to handle. He's upset my parents are selling, but it's not up to him." Chris glanced at his watch. "And now that you know more about my family than I'm sure you ever really wanted to know, the one thing I can't tell you is where Kevin is. I haven't seen him today."

"That's okay." She glanced at Bert, who was snapping photos of the dock. "I'll take my chances with one of Apple Station's finest."

"Alright. It was nice to meet you," Chris said as Jenn nodded in agreement.

"Likewise."

They parted ways, and as Olivia walked toward the dock, her phone played the first few bars of "I Shot the Sheriff." She eyed the photo of her Texas Ranger teddy bear on the screen.

"Hello. Olivia Penn speaking."

"Where are you?" Preston asked.

"I'm at the lake," she replied, instantly regretting blurting out the imprudent response.

"Why are you there?"

She took a deep breath and counted to three, ready to choose her words more carefully.

"Save it, Olivia. Don't work too hard coming up with an excuse. I need you to come to the police station immediately."

"Why? What's going on?"

"Just get here as soon as you can."

CHAPTER 11

After Olivia arrived back in town, she parked in a visitor's spot beside the chief's cruiser in front of the police station. She had rewound yesterday's events several times on the way in, trying to recall any details that she may have missed telling Jayden. Her role, though, had been succinct, and her story had played out cut and dry. She closed her door as a postal worker passed by, and they exchanged cordial "good day" wishes. She inhaled a calming breath to settle her butterflies. Her best guess was that Preston's summons had something to do with the article in the newspaper.

She entered the station and remained in the lobby, waiting for someone to notice. A three-foot-tall wooden gate and an unoccupied reception desk separated the small foyer from the workroom. Payne was standing beside the station's holding cell speaking with Preston, while Cole and Bert were huddled around a computer.

Jayden was sitting at her desk, resting a phone loosely against her ear as if hunkered down on hold.

Olivia stepped to the swing gate, reluctant to cross the divide. She waved her hand at no one in particular. "Hello. I'm here. I came like you asked me to."

The room went silent as all heads swiveled toward her. She scanned the stares, feeling the spotlight, and resisted the urge to peek over her shoulder to see if someone had walked in behind her.

Payne locked on her for a moment and then turned back to Preston. "Let me know if Dana comes up with anything else." Then he stepped into his office, pushing the door shut behind him.

Preston waved Olivia over, and she walked through the gate and strode past the deputies, watching them as they watched her. "Here I am," she said to Preston. "What's so pressing that I'm on your speed dial today?"

He swiped a Manilla folder off the top of a file cabinet. "Come this way."

He led her down a short hallway, past four closed doors, and into the last room on the right. It was small with stark white walls and a sealed gray, concrete floor. There were no windows, mirrors, or clocks. Only a table, two chairs, and a video camera outfitted the confined room.

He shut the door and then sat at the table, motioning for her to do the same. "Please, grab a chair."

She remained standing by her only exit, shifting her eyes back and forth from him to the camera in the upper corner. "What's this about? I already told you everything I know from yesterday. If this is about the article in the paper, my involvement was exaggerated far beyond my consent."

"Olivia, please sit."

"Why do I feel I'm being questioned?"

He drummed his fingertips on the folder, sliding it slightly back and forth. "Why were you at the lake this morning?"

"Am I being questioned? Is that why I'm here? Because I was at the lake?"

He tilted his head and rubbed his chin but didn't part his lips. She had walked into this blind, and now, she had to play by his rules. She slid the metal folding chair toward her, scraping its uncapped tips across the scuffed floor. She lowered slowly and sat but moved no closer to the utilitarian table.

He opened the file and removed a single sheet of white paper with a crayon drawing. "I'm showing this to you off the record. What you see here and what we discuss isn't to find its way into a story for the newspaper. Do you agree with that?"

The cloak-and-dagger offer piqued her curiosity. "I do."

He turned the sheet around and slid it across the table toward her. "What does this look like to you?"

It was a simple picture drawn with fine tip crayons, using all eight of the classic colors. "This looks like something a child did."

"The drawing itself. What do you see?"

She glanced at him, gauging whether he was joking. "For real? Is this some new form of Rorschach?"

"No. Tell me what you see."

She leaned in and studied it as if cramming for a pop quiz. "Okay. In the center, that's a big semi-oval with blue squiggles. In the upper left here, those are two stick figures, no doubt. So, people. Two people. One has arms and legs and the other just has arms. Poor fella." She smiled, but his lack of mirroring refocused her efforts. "Okay. And next to them, this is another figure with possibly four legs. So, maybe an animal? How am I doing?"

"We're thinking it's a dog. Please, continue."

"Well, right below the two people and the stick figure you're calling a dog, in this bottom left corner ..." She gauged a pair of inch-long horizontal lines, each balanced on two circles. "Hmm. Clearly, neither people nor a dog. I can't even guess. But across from whatever it is, in this bottom right corner, this square with the semi-triangle on the top—I'd guess that's a house. And these two tall lines next to it with the red and orange streaks shooting from the top—those have got to be trees. Up here, in the top right corner, same thing. Another tree. Next to the tree, another stick figure. Arms and legs, good for him." She slid the paper back toward him. "Now, what's this about?"

He traced his finger around the oval and along a horizontal line that extended from its right side inward about two inches. "We think this is the lake, and this is the dock."

She scooted her chair closer. "Okay. I can see that. And on the dock is a stick figure that's missing legs, so again, another unfortunate person. And there, by the dock's shore, another four-legged figure. Similar to this one in the left corner. A little smaller, though. This squarish thing sitting at the end of the dock, no idea."

Preston pointed at a two-inch horizontal line with four short marks extending upward amid the blue squiggles.

She looked at him. "Okay. I think I see where you're going with this. I take it that's the victim by the macabre dead bug pose."

He nodded. "Possibly. Melissa Barns' son drew this."

"Mikey? He drew this. When?"

"Yesterday. After we had finished speaking, I left the park to go up to Melissa's house to find Jason. He was there, and I questioned Jason and Melissa separately in the kitchen. When I was through and on my way out, I passed Mikey in the living room, and he was working on this."

"Do you know he's on the autism spectrum? I'm lost at what you're getting at here and how any of this involves me." She peeked at the camera. "Is this being recorded?"

He pointed to the lower left corner. "We think these are cars. These two figures with the dog, possibly you and A.J." He traced his finger to the figure on the dock. "And then here, you again on the dock with your father's dog when you found the victim. The house we believe is Melissa's. Jayden has trained in helping traumatized children who have witnessed or been involved in crime. She says children will often draw their own house for a sense of security and comfort."

She placed her hand on the drawing. "Let me get this straight. You think Mikey saw A.J., me, and Buddy when we were at the lake, and then saw me again when I found the victim? But how does this make any sense? I'm over here, and then I'm over here. We are calling him the victim, right? So, you're thinking this is a suspicious death. Not an accident."

He leaned back, softening his jaw. "I don't know how much stock to put into this drawing, but there's a lot about it that seems to fit. We know he was there twice yesterday, once when he got out of the house—when you saw him with A.J.—and then again shortly after you found the body. Melissa tells us Mikey is mostly nonverbal. We don't have a good way to question him about what he witnessed. All we have is this drawing, but we can't pass it off as coincidence." He pointed at the upper right corner. "This troubles me."

She studied the tree and stick figure beside it. "Who is that supposed to be?"

"Exactly. Who is that? We think it's possible Mikey may have been watching someone, and that someone may have been watching you."

She leaned back in her chair, distancing herself from

the drawing. "I didn't see anyone else there. I told you that. We saw Kevin and Jason when we were there earlier, and that's it."

He swiped the paper toward him and then placed it in the folder. "We have to keep in mind that Mikey drew this. And though we can't explain everything happening in this picture, we can't dismiss it just because we don't understand. I think he's saying something here."

"I get that, but I have nothing more to tell you. I didn't see anyone else."

He picked up the file and tapped it twice on the table. "But someone may have thought that you did."

The knot in her stomach doubled as his words sunk in. "Okay. So, then what?"

"Is there someplace you can go until we figure this out?"

"Go? Go where? I'm not following."

"Can you get out of town? Maybe stay with some friends in D.C. for a while?"

"Wait. You think I'm in danger? What about Mikey? And his mom. A.J. was there, too."

"Kevin is checking in on Melissa and Mikey. I'll talk to A.J., but this drawing seems to show two moments of time, and the connection between those is you. First, when you were there with A.J., and then when you found the victim. A.J. isn't who I'm worried about."

"You can't be serious. Get out of town? I'm sure you can guess how I feel about that. Why would anyone want to kill some guy checking out an algae bloom, anyway?"

"That guy was Ethan Dunn, and as you know, he worked for the VDEQ."

"What was he doing at the dock that would make someone want to murder him?"

"I can't discuss those details with you. But if we can figure out the why, that may lead us to the who."

The door sprung open, spurring her to swivel in her seat. Jayden leaned into the interrogation room. "Detective, phone call."

He pushed back from the table and stood. "Give me a minute." He left the room, closing the door behind him.

She softened her gaze on the blank white wall facing her, replaying the scenes from yesterday. Nothing more came. She eyed the folder and then stared up at the camera for a count of five. *Shouldn't there be a red light? Is that even a thing?* She fingered the file, half-expecting Jayden to burst into the room and slap her hand away. Encountering no such resistance, she slid the folder toward her, peeked over her shoulder, and then removed the drawing.

A second look only confirmed the proposed narrative, though it didn't sit quite right with her. Preston's muffled voice grew louder and closer in the hallway. She snatched her phone out of her pocket, snapped a photo, and slid the folder back in place.

He opened the door and reentered the room. "Sorry about that."

She impishly smiled and winked at the camera and

then scooted away from the table and stood. "Are we done here?"

"Please consider what I asked. Be sure to lock your doors. Stay vigilant."

She saluted. "Aye, aye, captain. I will. I appreciate the concern, Detective Hills." She turned, exhaled a full breath, and walked out into the workroom.

"Hey, Olivia. Is everything okay?" Cole asked.

"Yes. Everything's fine. I guess you know what that was about."

He nodded. "Call us if you're concerned about anything."

"Thanks, I will." She paused, remembering she still lacked any official statement for Ellen. "Tell me, Cole. Is the investigation proceeding as if there's a threat to community safety? Does the town need to be worried that a murderer is on the loose? And what about the festival on Friday? Is that going to be canceled?"

"We're not calling it a murder, yet. The ME hasn't filed her final report. There's been no talk of canceling the activities. We always have increased security for town events, anyway. If the chief thinks there's any sort of risk, he'll advise the mayor to postpone. Otherwise, it's up to city hall, and they'll probably go with whatever the chief recommends."

"Hopefully, everything will be settled by then," she said. "Maybe this was just an accident. Will you and Bert be dressing up this year for the parade?"

"Definitely. We're reprising our convict costumes

from last year. We think we have a shot at winning first place again. Do you know whether Sophia is coming? We really hit it off at the spring festival."

She stifled a smile. "I believe she'll be there. She reminds me about that luncheon every chance she gets. I'll let her know that you've been asking about her. I'll see you later."

She turned to go, but paused at Jayden's desk. "What about you? Will you be joining Cole and Bert? Maybe play out a scene from *Con Air*?"

Jayden dead-eyed her, looking up from the computer screen. "What do you think?"

"Right. Gotcha." Olivia waved to Cole, and then left the station. She double-timed the steps, hopped into her Expedition, and set off straight back toward the lake. She wasn't about to run around the police to investigate the murder. However, if she was in danger, she wanted to know as much as she could about the risk. In the spring, she had made the mistake of being too trusting and complacent regarding her safety, and it had gotten her father hurt. She had promised herself never to put her family or friends in that situation again. The journalist in her sensed something fishy, and she wasn't about to sit idly by without at least trying to learn more about what Mikey saw at the lake.

CHAPTER 12

The narrow access road leading to Melissa's house sloped upward and wound through a dense forest of oak, maple, and hickory. The fading fall canopy scattered the soft afternoon sunlight, bathing the quiet lane with a tranquil glow. Olivia drove by a pop-up camper and waved at a hiker who was wrangling two Labradors and a Rottweiler. Farther up, she passed a single-wide mobile home with gray siding and a slanted, shingled roof. A weathered red pickup with a propped-up hood rested on a patch of matted grass along one of its sides. The road climbed steeper, and as she cornered the next bend, she came upon a quaint cottage with a small, covered porch and a front yard arrayed like a playground. A sand table, bicycle with training wheels, and jungle gym with a slide and swing promised hours of fun for any energetic kid.

She parked on a makeshift driveway behind a red EcoSport with a specialty "Unlocking Autism" DMV license plate. Two large windows with drawn back sheers flanked both sides of a screened-in steel-blue door. Behind the house, the forested land sloped down. The faint voices and laughter she heard hinted she was near to the trail that encircled the lake.

She walked onto the porch, peeked through the mesh screen that guarded the half-opened door, and gently rapped on the aluminum frame. Mikey popped up from a couch and galloped to where she was standing.

She leaned down and smiled as he gazed past her without saying a peep. "Hi, Mikey."

He turned, ran a few paces into the living room, and then skipped back toward the screen.

She tried again. "Hi, is your mommy here?"

He flicked his fingers and stared off to her side. Melissa came into view of the living room, drying her hands with a yellow checkered tea towel. "Who's there, Mikey?" she said.

"Hello. I'm Olivia Penn. I'm the one who saw Mikey by the lake yesterday. I was there when Kevin called you, and he mentioned that someone had seen him. That someone was me."

Melissa opened the front door wide, gauging her for a moment. "Oh. Mikey, go sit on the couch. Do your letters." He turned and skated back into the living room. She set the tea towel on a table near the entrance, reached up to the top of the screen, and slid open a latch. "I was trying to circulate some fresh air in here. Please come in."

She stepped inside as Melissa closed the door and then pointed a mini-remote at a small box installed above the doorknob. She slipped the remote into her pocket and then gestured toward the door. "It's an alarm. I have them on all the doors and windows for Mikey's safety. Sometimes he likes to venture outside on his own, and they alert me if he gets out. You must think I'm an awful mother."

"No, not at all. Why would you say that?"

"Jason told me you saw Mikey by himself at the lake yesterday. It was my fault. I accidentally dozed off on the couch when we were watching one of his cartoons, and I didn't have the front door alarm set. It's just that I've been so tired. He's homeschooled, and I work IT customer service from here after his bedtime. Sunday night was a rough one for both of us. He goes through spells when he doesn't sleep well."

"You don't need to explain anything to me. It sounds like you have more than enough reason to be exhausted."

Mikey grunted and dropped a children's tablet on the floor.

Melissa glanced toward the living room. "Mommy will just be a second."

He screamed and swiped a rectangular storage container off the coffee table. Then he climbed onto the couch and bounced, bending his knees without leaving his feet.

Melissa's shoulders slumped and rounded. "Mikey, stop that. Excuse me. Let me set him up with a video.

Come on Mikey, get down. Let's go watch the penguins."
She lifted him off the sofa and led him by the hand into a
hallway off the living room.

Olivia waited for a moment by the front door and
then eyed the items Mikey had strewn across the floor.
She glanced at the hallway and then stepped around the
couch and knelt, picking up the overturned bin. She
tidied up, setting a TV remote, the tablet, and a weighted
blue stuffed toy turtle on the coffee table. She gathered
crayons, building blocks, and metal-cast cars, placing
them all in the container. Melissa's purse lay upturned as
well, and while most of the contents had remained
secure, her keys and a prescription bottle had fallen out.
She placed the purse on the table and then spied a few
more items poking out from under the couch. She swept
her hand under as far as she could, gathering more
blocks, two squishy sensory balls, and three empty glass
vials. After depositing all the items in the container, she
stood and placed it on the table.

Melissa returned to the living room. "Okay, he's good
for a while. Oh, you didn't have to clean up."

"I thought I'd make myself useful. Your purse was on
the floor, and I think a couple of things fell out. I put
everything in the container."

Melissa grabbed her keys and the prescription bottle
out of the bin and stashed them in her purse. "Thank
you. I usually don't leave it there, but we were out earlier,
and I threw it on the table when we got back in. Mikey
was hungry, and I needed to fix him something to eat."

Olivia glanced toward the hallway. "Is he okay? I didn't mean to upset him."

"He's fine. It's not you. Sometimes it's just the slightest thing that sets him off." She bent over and picked up two building blocks that Olivia had missed. "These are his favorite. He loves stacking them. He likes the blue ones the best. I find them all over the house, in the yard, in his pockets. He puts everything in his pockets. I can't tell you how many times rocks and twigs have gone through the wash." She dropped the blocks into the bin and sighed. "Can I get you something? Coffee?"

"No, thank you. But it smells wonderful in here. Like Thanksgiving."

Melissa nodded. "An unexpected, early fall feast for us. I don't want to sound rude, but why exactly are you here?"

"I understand you talked to the police yesterday."

"That's right, but I don't know anything about what happened at the lake or about the man who died."

"The police showed me the picture that Mikey drew."

A vehicle's door slammed shut outside. Melissa glimpsed through the window, pulled the remote from her pocket, and turned off the alarm. She opened the front door, and Kevin stepped in.

"What are you doing here?" he asked Olivia.

Melissa placed her hand on his bicep. "She was asking about the police questioning me yesterday and about Mikey's drawing."

He glared at Olivia and then looked back at Melissa. "You know she's a reporter."

Olivia held up her hands and stepped toward them. "I'm not. I'm just trying—"

"Really? Because it was your picture on the front page of the paper this morning. Have you come here fishing for information? Melissa likes her privacy. I'm sure you can understand with Mikey's needs. He doesn't need disruption in his life."

"That's not what I'm doing. That's not why I came."

"I think you should leave," he said.

"Kevin. She was just asking about the drawing."

Olivia moved toward the door. "No, it's okay. I'm going. I'm sorry if I upset Mikey. It was nice to meet you, Melissa."

She exited the house, and Kevin followed closely behind. When she got out of earshot of the porch, she spun and squared up to him. "Look, I'm not trying to get any angle here or cause any problems."

He pointed a finger at her. "Stay away from her and Mikey."

"Ranger Rick!" Jason yelled.

They both turned toward Jason as he strolled up the lane. He cut through the front yard, skirting the jungle gym, and stopped an arm's length from them.

Kevin holstered his hands on his hips and scowled. "What do you want, Jason?"

He flashed a baiting smile. "I came to check on Melissa and Mikey."

"They're both fine. You can leave," Kevin said.

"I'd like to see for myself, if you don't mind."

Kevin stepped toward him. "I do mind. Tell me, Jason, what were you really doing down by the lake when you happened across that raccoon yesterday? Did you talk to that fieldworker? What did he say to you?"

"I don't have to answer your questions."

"Did he tell you that the park was going to be shut down until the bloom cleared? Did he tell you he had planned to test the entire area for toxins? Do you give discounts on the ginseng you poach if it's grown on contaminated land? Or could you no longer sell it? How much would that cost you?"

"I don't know what you're talking about, ranger. And it's not rocket science. That bloom is from your parents' farm. Is that what that guy said to you?"

Kevin launched at him, shoving Jason's shoulder and balling his hand into a fist. Olivia hooked Kevin's arm, trying her best to prevent an assault and battery.

"Hey! Stop. Everyone, relax," she said.

Jason smirked and stepped away, holding his hands up high. "Don't get your panties in a bunch, ranger. We all know what happens when you get angry. Tell Melissa I said hi." He pivoted around and sauntered through the yard and back down the lane.

Olivia lightened and then released her hold on Kevin's arm when he had eased his stance. "Are you okay?" she asked.

He narrowed his eyes and rubbed his jaw as if Jason

had punched his chin. "Leave Melissa alone." He strode to his SUV and then turned toward her before he got in. "My family had nothing to do with any of this. Print that in your paper." He slammed the door, reversed the truck, and kicked up dust and gravel as he sped away.

CHAPTER 13

Olivia arrived back in town at one o'clock and parked shop-side, a few suites down from the newspaper's office. She lingered behind the wheel, staring at the police station and feeling déjà vu. The morning hadn't gone according to plan. She now was involved in the investigation, but not in the way the paper's story had suggested. She had gathered no information from the police that she could share with Ellen to be printed. Further, her foray to Melissa's had proven futile as Kevin's temper had cut short her speculative visit.

She strolled down the block and opened the door to the newspaper's office as a middle-aged woman was leaving. Olivia stepped to her right to let her pass, only to be mirrored by the visitor, who shifted left. Each simultaneously reversed course, and then they danced around one another, shimmying out of the other's way.

The workroom was quiet and empty except for

Cooper, who was typing on a laptop at Paige's former desk. "Hey, Cooper." She pointed to Ellen's closed office door.

"She's not in. You can sit here." He stood and picked up his coffee cup. "I went to Jillian's for lunch, and there's an extra sandwich in the fridge. She had a two for Tuesday special today, but I'm stuffed. I feel like a turducken. It's honey-baked ham with mustard and provolone on ciabatta."

She beelined for the mini fridge in the back corner. "I adore you, Cooper, and I owe you a lunch. Next week, we'll go. Don't move on my account. I won't be here long. I can sit someplace else." She grabbed the sandwich and a bottle of water.

"It's okay. I don't mind. Sometimes, I just like working at Paige's desk. I still think of it as hers." He binned his coffee cup and held the rolling chair steady for her.

She sat at the desk, placing her food and drink in front of her. "Thanks, Cooper. You're a true gentleman. Are you sure you don't need this laptop?"

"That's how my mom raised me. The laptop is all yours. Are you writing something for the paper about the murder?"

She opened a browser. "Not exactly. The police aren't calling it a murder yet."

He pushed his Clark Kent glasses from the tip to the bridge of his nose. "This totally has *Murder She Wrote* all over it." He paused, taking a sip of coffee, and then continued. "That woman who just left was from Canada. Saskatchewan."

She typed "algae blooms" into the search box. "Okay. Good to know."

"Yeah, she came here looking for Cassandra."

She clicked on the first result and then peeked up at him. "Oh, really? What did she want?"

"She said she spoke with Cassandra at the end of May, just about the time everything went down with Grove Manor. She has an aunt who lives in Ben ... Benton—"

"Bentonville?"

"Yeah, that's it. Bentonville. You know where that is?"

"It's in Warren County, about forty minutes from here."

"That'll be my random fact for today. I use apps to learn a new piece of trivia, vocabulary word, and Spanish phrase every day. Me gusta el chocolate. That means I like chocolate. Anyway, she said she talked with Cassandra about making apple butter, of all things. I love apple butter. I didn't know Cassandra made it."

"Me either. I'm sure Cassandra will be sorry she missed her. Bad timing. What are the odds?"

She focused back on the screen and resumed her search. She spent the next thirty minutes eating her freebie sandwich and researching the causes, effects, testing, and monitoring of algae blooms. She opened a tab for a map of the lake, studied it, and zoomed out for a wider view. Fields Farm abutted the parkland along its northeastern aspect while Whispering Meadows Country Club bordered its northwestern edge.

She sniffed at a hint of lavender and then glanced over her shoulder as Cooper leaned down close to her ear. "Do you need something from me?" she said. "Do you smell lavender?"

"It's my new hand cream. The bottle is on my desk if you wanna try it. It's from the farm out near Catlett that you told me about. They also have a lovely lavender-vanilla lotion you'd like." He drew a vague circle with his finger around the lake on the map. "I see what you're doing. Sort of. Have you devised any theories?"

She switched the map to a satellite view and layered over labels for locations, routes, and points of interest. "No." She leaned back in her chair and then looked up at him. "I read your contributions to the article in the paper this morning."

He straightened and beamed. "Pretty good, huh?"

"Writing-wise, thumbs-up. Content-wise, no, because I don't have suspicions—yet. I'm not even officially covering the investigation."

He bent forward and drew closer to the screen. "I didn't realize the golf course was that big. No wonder they're trying to get that tournament."

"Who are 'they,' and what tournament are you talking about?"

"Philip Wayne. He owns the country club. He's been lobbying the national pro tour to have his club selected as a host for an annual event. He's been doing all kinds of upgrades to the greens and facilities. They're building a conference center and a luxury hotel, too. It's a big deal if the club becomes a pro tour stop. It would be exciting to have something like that around here. We could get nationwide media coverage. Imagine, Apple Station mentioned on ESPN."

She slowly swiveled her chair back and forth. "You may be onto something. I bet that kind of golf tournament would bring in big money."

"Sure would. I remember Paige told me about it when Whispering Meadows Winery opened last year. She covered a VIP tasting event they held a few days before the official launch. The winery and vineyard are part of a five-year expansion plan that includes construction of the conference center and hotel. I wrote the caption copy for the photo we ran for Paige's story, using a quote from Ben Billingsley. He said he wanted Whispering Meadows to become an international destination."

"Billingsley?" She tensed at the mention of the questionable lawyer who had helped A.J. navigate legal troubles five months ago, in May. "How is he involved?"

"He and Philip Wayne are business partners in the winery."

She tilted the laptop toward him. "Show me where the winery and vineyards are on the map."

He used the track pad to locate, zoom in, and recenter the image. "Thereabouts."

"That's pretty close to Fields Farm." She pointed to the land next to the winery. "This acreage here looks like it would be part of the farm. Do you know if their crop fields extend that far back on the property?"

"They do. I volunteer during their fall festival season to help Mrs. Fields when they have school groups come in on weekdays for the corn maze. She always gives me a pumpkin pie to take home. Sometimes she puts chocolate chips or pecans in. I get whipped topping—you know, the canned stuff with those nozzles that you can shoot straight into your mouth—"

"Stay with me for a second, Cooper. Talk to me about the fields."

"Some days after my shift, I meet up with a friend of mine who works there, and I ride around the farm with her as she does some of her checks and chores. I don't know if anything is growing on the back acreage now because they've completed their summer harvest and a lot of their fields are bare."

"You're sure all that land is arable?"

"If that means you can grow crops on it, I think so. Their operation is huge. Why? What are you thinking?"

"You're telling me that Philip Wayne wants his country club to become a tour stop and an international destination for big spenders. His winery and vineyards are next to fertile land that's for sale. That sounds like a business opportunity to me."

Cooper nudged her. "Sugar plum fairies. I see where you're going with this. Clever. And you said you weren't investigating. I knew it. You're just like Paige when you smell a story."

She grinned, nudging him back. "Thanks, Cooper. That's about the best thing you could ever say to me."

"What's your next move, chief?"

She shut the laptop, binned her trash, and stood. "It's time for a field trip."

CHAPTER 14

Whispering Meadows was a mere ten miles outside of Apple Station, though it seemed a world away from the cozy charm of small-town life. She had driven past the sprawling, stately grounds many times on her way to Sky Meadows State Park, but she never had mustered the curiosity to stop. The two-lane road leading to the stonewall entrance was lined with the paddock-style wood fencing that was ubiquitous in the rolling hills of Virginia's horse country.

The country club was nonexclusive, offering fine dining, spa treatments, and recreational activities to lure visitors throughout the four seasons. Paying members received privileges, including discounted amenities, prime tee times, and invitations to private events.

Olivia turned onto the property and drove toward the clubhouse along a lane lined with elm trees. She passed a riding arena set ready for equestrian training, with four horses saddled in the ring. Support staff were spreading out cross bar, vertical, and wall jumps evenly in sequence. A group of junior equestrians had gathered around a svelte woman sporting English riding apparel, who was speaking while pointing out various areas in the arena. Two Canadian geese waddled onto the road in front of Olivia, and she and an outbound Cadillac Escalade both slowed and then stopped, waiting for the pair to cross.

The country estate clubhouse sat at the top of a small crest of land that overlooked a portion of the golf course behind it. The long, opulent manor was multi-tiered and had a turret on one of its front corners. She counted five chimneys, four entrances, and at least fifteen windows on each floor.

She parked on the outskirts of the lot, planning to scope out the lay of the land on her extended walk to the clubhouse. The foot traffic skewed retiree in the early afternoon hour. Players wheeled their golf carts to and from the lot, loading and unloading their clubs from their luxury or chauffeured vehicles. She strolled by the main entrance and toward the turret corner, imagining its three tiers of wraparound windows would make it the perfect reading room. A wide, circular putting green was situated a chip shot from where she stood on the sidewalk. Several players were hunched over their putters, gauging distances and taking turns practicing their short game. The view beyond stretched over the golf course's opening tee, manicured fairways, and verdant greens.

"Excuse me, miss," a man behind her said.

She spun to face a broad-shouldered hunk with biceps ready to burst his polo shirt's short sleeves. His slim-fit khakis divulged daily leg squats, and his close-cropped hair complied with the strictest of military regulations. He tapped his name tag. "I'm Rhett. You look like you're searching for someone. Can I help you?"

She glanced at the gleaming gold badge on his protruding pec. Golf pro. Though a flurry of flirtatious thoughts flooded her mind, she went with the least interesting and most practical answer in the moment. "I'm looking for Philip Wayne."

He winked as his sparkling smile and warm, deep voice eased over her like melted butter. "The best chance of finding him is to look in the clubhouse. If you go right through that entrance, just ask at the concierge desk. Would you like me to show you?"

She drank in his twinkling ocean-blue eyes, lingering for a moment before refocusing. "Thanks. I'll find my way."

The sliding glass doors parted as she approached, revealing a lavish, grand lobby. A concierge wrapped in a black pencil skirt suit scuttled around the reception counter and cordially greeted her as though she were a club VIP.

"Welcome to Whispering Meadows. How can I be of service to you today?"

"I was hoping to speak with——"

"Ms. Penn," a familiar voice behind her said.

She turned as Ben Billingsley strolled across the lobby

with a man who was sporting a Whispering Pines navy polo and finely tailored steel-gray pants.

"I didn't know you were a member here," Ben said. "Philip, this is Olivia Penn."

Philip Wayne considered her for a moment and then lit up, snapping his fingers. "Of course. I recognize the name. You were involved in that Grove Manor business. How terrifying that must've been for you. Small towns and their secrets. You got injured, didn't you?"

"Yes, but I'm fine now."

"That's good to hear. Whatever happened to that property?" Philip asked.

She glanced at Ben, who showed no signs of offering any details. "The new owner settled the tax lien. He's developing a portion of it and selling select parcels."

"Wise move in this market," Philip replied. "Are you enjoying your day at Whispering Meadows? You're a member here, aren't you? We won't have too many more days like this to play a round of golf before winter comes."

"Oh, no. I'm not a member."

"Then I consider it my mission to convince you to join us. Do you golf?"

"No. Not yet."

"We have some of the finest pros for coaches. All the instruction is one-on-one to address your personal needs. If golf isn't your thing, we also have a world-class spa and a five-star restaurant. This Sunday, I'm hosting a private tasting event at the winery. Bring your husband. I'll add your name to my guest list."

"That's kind of you, but I'm not sure of my plans right now."

Philip's smooth, genuine smile oozed a charisma that no doubt had greased and sealed many successful business negotiations. She guessed he was in his late sixties, though he appeared much younger with his thick, silver-gray hair and Copacabana tan.

"Don't say no. Just think about it."

"Please, sir. Wait!" the concierge begged from the entrance of the lobby.

The three turned at once as Chris stormed straight for them while pointing an accusatory finger. "Wayne!"

The concierge chased after him, click-clacking with staccato steps. As the gap widened, though, she retreated to her desk, reached over the counter, and grabbed a phone.

Chris slowed and then stopped once he was within shoving distance. "You're poisoning our land."

Philip stood without flinching, fully unfazed. "Mr. Fields, a pleasure to see you. What is it you think I'm doing?"

"Your chemicals are leaching onto our property. Last year, we almost lost our organic certification because of you, and now, you're doing it again. You're responsible for that bloom at the lake."

Philip kept cool, steepling his hands. "Mr. Fields, we are stewards of the land. The environment's health is our top priority. We dedicate ourselves to conservation and the use of renewable energy sources. We gear all our efforts toward ensuring the ecosystem's well-being so that we may enjoy nature's beauty for years to come."

"You're full of it. I've been around the pond on the thirteenth hole. You have algae growth and dead fish there, the same as in the lake."

"Let me first thank you for being a member, Mr. Fields. Your parents represent the finest of Apple Station. I can assure you, though, that there is no relation between the two. A highly trained crew tests our soil regularly and inspects our irrigation system daily. We're not an organic golf course, but we use only the formulations the EPA allows, in the quantities that are permitted. We are one hundred percent within the target ranges. Our compliance follows best practice guidelines and is on par with the highest standards."

The concierge approached with a firm, steely stride. "Mr. Wayne, security is on their way."

He nodded. "Thank you, Ms. Butler."

Ben stepped toward Chris. "I think you should leave before security arrives."

Philip closed the distance. "It's okay, Ben. Mr. Fields, nobody has to be a genius to figure out what's occurring here. Tell me, what happens if your buyers test your parents' farm for contaminants prior to the sale? I bet that bloom at Lake Crystal has put a bug in their ear. Is anyone going to buy the land when it comes handcuffed

SILENCE SAYS THE MOST

with millions in fines? How is it that the market value of your parents' property grew fifteen percent in one year?"

A security guard jogged through the lobby, hustling over to the group. He wedged himself between Philip and Chris. "Sir, you'll need to leave now."

Philip stepped out from behind the guard. "Thank you, Blake. Just one moment. Mr. Fields, tell your parents that my offer still stands. I'll buy those back five acres, full ask, all cash, right now. You convince them to take it before I withdraw the offer. I wouldn't want to buy any land known to be contaminated. That would ruin my reputation and go against everything we stand for here at Whispering Meadows."

The security guard grabbed Chris' arm and pulled him away. "Time to leave, sir."

Philip's eyes narrowed. "Thank you for stopping by, Mr. Fields. Blake, make sure he gets a bottle of Chardonnay from my personal stock."

Chris tried to shrug off the guard's hold but remained snared until he was out of the door and clear of the entrance.

CHAPTER 15

Philip turned, sparked his magnetic smile, and refocused on Olivia. "Please don't allow the behavior of one individual to taint your view of the experience we create for our guests. When you visit Whispering Meadows, my aim is to ensure that you rest, relax, and restore. Business sometimes makes blood run high. It's never personal. Of course, all of Mr. Fields' allegations are untrue."

Ms. Butler timidly approached with soft heel clicks and waited until Philip invited her to speak. "Mr. Wayne, I'm so sorry. He barged in, and I tried to stop him."

"No need to apologize, Ms. Butler. I wouldn't have wanted you to be in his way. Mr. Fields was out of line, but you handled the unfortunate situation with poise. Thank you for calling security so quickly."

She forced a pained half-smile, seemingly embarrassed by the compliment for something she felt the need to apologize for. "Everyone is ready for you in the board-room, Mr. Wayne. Should I tell them you'll be late?"

"No. We'll be right in. Ms. Penn, it was a pleasure to meet you, and I'm glad that you're well. Ben and I have business to attend to. Please consider joining us as a member. Why don't you stick around for a while and enjoy our grounds and the clubhouse as my guest today. Ms. Butler, add Ms. Penn and a plus one on my VIP list for the tasting event at the winery this weekend."

Ms. Butler bobbed her head and grinned as if the request had just made her day. "My pleasure." She bustled off, no doubt to address the matter immediately.

"Now, please excuse us." Philip extended his hand, inviting Ben to lead the way to their meeting.

Olivia pivoted to exit and then politely waved to Ms. Butler as she passed the concierge desk. The twin doors swished aside, ushering her from the embrace of the lavish lobby. Though she was more apt to be lounging on a blanket while enjoying a picnic lunch, the lure of luxury was seductive. Everything about the clubhouse was as warm and welcoming as Beverly's inn. Rather than being treated as though she didn't belong, Philip had made her feel as though she fit right in. She skipped ahead to the weekend. *Wine tasting with a plus one. Could be fun. Golf ... definitely, would need lessons. Lots of lessons ... with golf pro Rhett.*

The doors swooshed and clapped shut, snapping her out of fantasyland. Payne's cruiser and Preston's truck were driving through the parking lot, heading straight for the main entrance. She turned and bolted toward the putting green. Remaining unseen would mean not having to come up with an explanation for her presence, and she was okey dokey with forgoing any further interaction with the police.

She quickstepped her way along the sidewalk and cut across the grass to skirt the clubhouse's turret corner until she was no longer in the line of sight of the main entrance. A walkway ran parallel to a delivery road that sloped down and wound toward the rear of the club-house. Betting on what goes around comes around, she followed the sidewalk to circle the back of the building to access the parking lot's other end.

The sidewalk flattened as it tucked under a spacious observatory deck that offered a vista of the front fairways. The clubhouse's loading dock was bustling with deliveries. As soon as one box truck pulled out, another reversed in, readying to offload goods. Workers flitted back and forth through the open bay doors, hauling crates, or using dollies to bring in the cartons that were too heavy to carry.

As she'd suspected, the walkway continued around to the clubhouse's opposite side. She slowed and then stopped, waiting for a cargo van to pull out of a delivery zone. An employee in a golf cart zipped by her and drove fifty yards up a narrow service road to a steel-arched storage shed. The driver hopped out of the cart and dashed inside. He quickly reappeared with a white bag slung over his shoulder and dumped it into the golf cart's rear carry bin. In no time, he reversed and returned the way he had come, cruising by without paying a lick of attention to her.

She weighed the distance to the shed and then watched the workers busy by the dock. She paced backward a few steps, gauging whether anyone had noticed, and when no eyes turned toward her, she pivoted and went for it. She strode confidently at a steady pace and peeked over her shoulder only once as she neared the maintenance shed.

The grounds crew worker had left the square-cut, roll-up door open. She surmised this was probably standard fare, as the staff would need to come and go for supplies and equipment throughout the day. She wasted no time and stepped inside without hesitating.

The acrid smell of chemical fertilizer assaulted her sinuses instantly. She squinted, trying to quell her eyes' quick tears and burning irritation. A metallic taste and tickle in her throat triggered a coughing fit that left her short of breath. Two industrial floor fans by the entrance sat idle, allowing the air to stagnate as still as death. She wiped the water from her eyes and slowed her breathing, taking a minute more to acclimate.

The full length of the shed's right side was lined with landscaping equipment. Lawn mowers, leaf blowers, and hedge trimmers sat in tidy rows toward the rear. Chain saws, pump sprayers, and fertilizer spreaders were stored in the middle. A rolling tool chest sat beside two worktables situated for ease of access at the front.

On the left side and all along the back wall, plastic bags of landscaping products had been piled high on wooden pallets. The first three stacks were types of grass: Bermuda, zoysia, and rye. She slid her phone out of her pocket and worked her way to the back, photographing all visible labels.

Nondescript white bags ladened the remaining pallets, each identified by a series of three numbers: 18-4-18, 15-0-0, 12-0-0. In the rear corner, two rows of six five-gallon jugs of 2-0-16 sat neatly aligned. She squatted, snapping a photo of the containers, and then stood abruptly to leave. A chemical-induced wave of nausea soured her stomach and foreboding spots blurred her visual field.

She pocketed her phone, aiming to exit before her impromptu look-see left her flat on her back, staring helplessly at the ceiling. She turned, took two steps, and stopped as Blake blocked the entranceway.

"What are you doing in here?" he asked.

She took a deep breath, coughed, and held up a finger to beg for a minute's reprieve. She wiped the water from her eyes again while quickly recalibrating. "Hi. I was admiring the grounds at Mr. Wayne's invitation. He makes a persuasive case for joining as a member. Anyway, I was walking about, and nature called. I came in here looking for a restroom, but clearly, I was mistaken. So, I think I'll just go back up to the clubhouse." She stepped toward daylight, pointing to his side. "I can scooch right by you there."

He shifted slightly to block her, removed his phone from his pants pocket, and tapped the screen twice. "Mr. Wayne, this is Blake over in maintenance shed one. We have a situation here. There's a woman looking around—"

"No. I was searching for a restroom. Really, I can just go. Sorry to bother you." She coughed again, side-stepped, and braced herself on the doorframe.

He stared at her while listening to Philip. "Okay, right away, Mr. Wayne. We're on our way in." He ended the call and pocketed his cell. "Ma'am, you'll need to come with me."

CHAPTER 16

Blake escorted Olivia along the service road that wound back to the clubhouse, shadowing her as though she was a fugitive about to take flight. She was relieved at least to be out of the shed and breathing fresh air. Her headache and brain fog were dissipating, and her legs had steadied and the wooziness cleared.

As they neared the loading dock, she slowed and appealed to him with a last-ditch plea. "This is all a silly misunderstanding. I got turned around on the grounds, and I thought there may be a restroom for employees inside the maintenance shed." She gestured vaguely toward the walkway that skirted the side of the clubhouse, leading to the parking lot. "My car is right up there. I can just leave. Mr. Wayne has much more important business to deal with than somebody who doesn't know where they're going."

He pointed to the rear of the building, where a

supplier was reversing a box truck with Maryland license plates to an off-loading dock. "We can enter through the employee entrance."

Once inside, he assumed the point, guiding her through a maze of plain-Jane hallways that bore no likeness to the lobby's opulence. He propped open a swing door with his fingertips, leading into the clubhouse's commercial-sized kitchen. Shiny stainless-steel appliances lined the walls from end to end. Staff attired in their immaculate culinary whites silently prepped ingredients at evenly spaced workstations. They kept their heads down, peeling potatoes, parsnips, and carrots loaded on half-sheet pans in front of them.

After passing through the kitchen, they ascended a flight of stairs into the clubhouse's main dining room. A barkeep tended to the wall behind his counter, meticulously turning bottles to show off their labels. Other staff members readied the round walnut-wood tables, aligning place settings on pressed linens with precision. Mini bouquets of fresh fall blooms adorned the center of each table, and a waiter dressed in black filled their fluted vases with water.

Blake steered her straight to a private banquet room off the main dining floor. She opened the door, stepped inside, and killed her stride. Philip stood near a podium, speaking with Payne and Preston. As both officers turned, she let loose a silent stream of salty language in her head that would make a pirate proud.

Philip smiled, drawing his eyebrows together. "Ms.

Penn, I'm sorry. I misunderstood the situation. Blake called, reporting a trespasser. He didn't mention you by name."

She glanced at Preston, sensing his stare. "Please, you can call me Olivia."

"I found her in the maintenance shed behind the clubhouse, looking around."

She paced a few timid steps forward, raising her hand slightly. "Let me clarify that. I was searching for a restroom."

Payne crossed his arms. "In a storage shed?"

"It's okay, Ray. She's my guest. I invited her to enjoy the grounds."

"Are you a member here?" Payne asked.

She half-smiled, peeking again at Preston. "No, not yet. Maybe one day? This is just a misunderstanding."

"What am I misunderstanding about security finding you in a private maintenance shed, Ms. Penn?" Payne said. "Is that normal, Philip, for your guests to be in and out of your maintenance buildings?"

"No. But I hardly think she was doing anything wrong."

"Sounds like she was trespassing to me, and that's wrong and suspicious in my eyes."

Preston turned slightly toward Payne. "No. I don't believe that's what's going on here."

"Do you want to press charges, Philip?" Payne asked.

"No, of course not. Come on now. You're blowing this out of proportion, Ray."

SILENCE SAYS THE MOST

"I don't think so, Philip. I would like to know what Ms. Penn was doing where she didn't belong." He stepped closer. "What are you really doing here and why are you interfering in a police matter?"

"I'm not interfering with anything."

He considered her for a moment more. "We'll need to take a ride to the station and have a talk."

"What? I didn't do anything. I'm not going anywhere with you."

"Is that so?" He stared at her for a count of three. "You're being detained for questioning. Detective, take her out to my vehicle."

She swiveled toward Preston, and he turned to Payne. "I don't think we need to take her anywhere. It seems she lost her sense of direction."

"Detective, I gave you an order. Put her in my car while I finish up in here." He tossed Preston his keys.

He caught the ring, and then lightly grasped her forearm, prodding her toward the door. "Let's go."

He pressed her out into the main dining room, and then once they were in the lobby, she yanked her elbow away. Ms. Butler was speaking with two patrons outside in front of the twin sliding doors. With no other prying eyes around, he steered her into a hallway near the concierge's counter.

"Hey! What are you doing? Let go of me."

He turned and drew in close. "Why are you here, Olivia?"

"I told you."

"Is that how you want to play this? Because I can't help you if I don't know what's going on. I don't think it's a coincidence that you showed up here right before we did. Tell me what you're doing here."

"What are *you* doing here?"

He shook his head and sighed. "No, Olivia. That's not how this works."

She peeked down the hallway and lowered her voice. "Did you know Fields Farm almost lost their organic certification last year? Chris seems to think that the chemicals used here at the country club for the golf course had something to do with it. Something from here may be causing the bloom at the lake, and the bloom and your victim have got to be connected."

He inched closer, enlivening the narrow space between them with a hint of sandalwood. "Stop, Olivia. Is this your idea of not getting involved?" Before she could counter, he gently grasped her elbow and led her back toward the lobby.

As soon as they were outside, he withdrew his hand, and they marched to Payne's cruiser as if they were a disgruntled couple. He opened the door, and she slid into the backseat. He leaned down, but she stared straight ahead, refusing to look at him.

"Payne is trying to rattle you. Don't say a word. I'll be right behind you. Let me handle him. Got it?"

Before she could even form a thought, he slammed the door and left her to stew in the back of a police car for the first time in her life.

CHAPTER 17

The ride back into town was as silent as the grave. Payne seemed to have as little inclination to speak to Olivia as she did to him. They parked in front of the police station, and she seethed as Payne and Preston debated on the sidewalk for five minutes on what should be done with her, as if she couldn't hear everything that was being said. Payne finally ripped the door open and ordered her out. Preston lent a hand to assist her from the backseat, and as she stood, her eyes pleaded with him for help.

Payne led the way into the station, jabbing his thumb toward the cell without breaking his stride. "Put her in there. I'll deal with her later." Then he walked into his office and slammed the door shut behind him.

Cole scurried around his desk as Preston unlocked the cell. "What's going on? You're not going to put her in there, are you?"

She stepped inside, and he clanged the steel bars

shut. He looked over at Cole. "Did you hear from the VDEQ?"

Cole wrinkled his brow and pivoted toward his desk. "Yes. I wrote the contact's name and number on a slip of paper. It's here someplace."

Preston leaned closer to the cell. "Sit tight."

She spread her arms wide as if taking in the refinement of luxurious confines. "That's brilliant, Detective. Outstanding advice."

Jayden smirked, watching the scene from her desk a few feet away.

Olivia glared at her. "What? You have something to say?"

Jayden shook her head. "No, ma'am. Let me know when you want your phone call."

Preston snatched a sticky note from Cole and entered Payne's office without bothering to knock. She plunked down on the cot and then flipped onto her back in a huff, crossing her arms and closing her eyes. Payne and Preston exchanged heated volleys and after five minutes, the muffled voices droned and faded as she softened into the cot topper's thin padding. Her breathing slowed, and she felt herself slipping into sleep.

The canoe bobbed gently as she smiled at A.J. under the cozy, cotton-ball clouds of the midday summer sky. A resident eagle soared from one treetop to another, never venturing far from its life-long mate. She marveled at the grace and strength of the majestic flight and turned toward A.J. "Did you see—A.J. A.J?" She stood, panicked, rocking the canoe in a wild rhythm as she searched the murky lake.

"Where is she?" a voice intoned.

She dropped to her knees and plunged her hand into the water, frantically grabbing to gain purchase on anything solid.

"Where is she?" the voice repeated.

"A.J., I'm here!" A wave crested over the bow, throwing her off balance and plunging her into the water, deeper and deeper. She inhaled sharply as the lake filled her lungs, and then her eyes popped open, and she bolted straight up off the cot.

"Where is she?" her father said.

She scanned the room as her heartbeat jackhammered. *Police station. I'm at the police station. It was a dream.*

"There she is. There's my favorite, one and only daughter." Her father pushed the swing gate aside and walked into the workroom.

"Dad? What are you doing here?"

"Word's out that you've been arrested," he said with a smirk. "And you told me you weren't going to snoop around."

"I wasn't snooping, and I wasn't arrested. What time is it?"

"Almost six."

"What? Why didn't someone wake me?" she said to no one in particular. "Where's Preston? Why am I still in here?"

Cole looked up from his desk. "Chief and Preston left."

She turned toward her dad. "Who called you?"

"Cooper texted me. He said he heard about your arrest on the scanner."

She grabbed the bars with both hands. "Why does Cooper have your number? And since when do you two text each other? I haven't been arrested. How could Preston have left me in here? This isn't happening. This isn't happening."

He patted her hand, offering a sympathetic smile. "I don't know, honey, you're in a jail cell. This seems to be happening. Maybe you're still in shock. This is a great opportunity for me, though. I finally have a good story to share on Friday when I go to the Elks. I can't wait to tell my friends about how I had to bail out my troubled daughter after she got herself arrested. I bet I'll get some free beers out of this. Everyone at the bar can relate when children go astray."

"Dad, this isn't funny. And I haven't been arrested."

He removed his cell from his pocket. "Ed's son is now wearing one of those ankle monitors." He lowered his voice. "Roy's daughter. Rehab. Twice. I'd like a picture." He lifted his phone, lining up a shot.

"Dad! Don't!"

"How do you zoom in on this thing?"

Jayden popped up from her chair. "Let me show you. You should shoot a video, too."

She could feel her cheeks turning volcanic. "Dad! Put that away!"

He pursed his lips, lowered the phone, and slipped it into his pocket. He turned toward Jayden. "Does she have a mug shot? Has bail been set? I bet it's a million bucks. You're worth it, honey."

She grunted and slumped down on the cot, burying her face in her hands and wanting everyone to go away.

"She's right," Jayden said. "She hasn't been arrested, just detained."

Olivia sprung up. "Thank you. Now, when can I get out of here?"

Jayden's desk phone rang, and she turned to answer it.

Her father leaned against the cell. "If you need to stay overnight, I can bring you a toothbrush and a change in clothes."

She clenched her teeth. "I'm not staying overnight."

Jayden sidled over and opened the door. "You're free to go."

She stormed out without waiting for her father. Once outside, the cool air calmed her, and she slowed her pace until he had caught up, and then they walked side by side.

"Come on," he said. "Let's get you home."

She tipped her head back and moaned. "The Expedition is at Whispering Meadows."

He wrapped an arm around her shoulders and kissed her cheek. "Don't worry about your car right now. You know, I was just kidding about everything. If Payne had been here, I would've punched him in the mouth for putting you in that cell."

She gave him a smile. "I'm glad it didn't come to that. Or we might've been sharing Apple Station's finest accommodations overnight."

"That's what fathers are for. I don't think you should go back to Whispering Meadows tonight. Let me take you home. How about we first stop up the street for an ice-cream cone? That'll make you feel better about almost getting arrested."

"I don't want ice cream. I just want to get home."

He pulled her in close with a side hug as they strolled along the sidewalk toward his Escape. "Ice cream would make me feel better. Fudge ripple or French vanilla. I've had a traumatic day, with having to come and get you out of jail."

"Dad, please don't—"

"I'm joking. Everything's okay. You're going to be okay. Nobody has filed any charges. Serves you right anyway for snooping around."

She shuffled along like a six-year-old caught with her hand in the cookie jar. "I wasn't snooping around. I was looking for a bathroom."

He snickered. "So that's your story?"

"And I'm sticking to it."

"That's my girl." He opened the car door for her, and once she was seated, he got in the driver's side. "I'll drop you off at home, and then I'll call A.J. to see if he can go out with me and pick up your car. I'll run him back here afterwards. Leave your key with me."

She slipped her keys out of her pocket, detached the fob for her Expedition from the ring, and laid it in the cupholder. He pulled away from the curb, passing Sophia's closed clinic, and headed out of town. On the way home, she spun an edited version of what had happened, stretching out the story for the length of the ride. He reiterated his concern about her getting involved in the case, and she countered she wasn't interfering with the police investigation and wouldn't further jeopardize a criminal record for the sake of a story.

He turned into the driveway, setting off the motion sensor for the front porch light. The living room was lit by a pair of tabletop lamps that welcomed them home with a warm, comforting glow. Her only agenda for the rest of the night was to sink into the couch and wait for it to swallow her whole. Until then, she would binge-watch something on TV that had nothing to do with mystery, crime, or doing time.

As she eased out of the car, he leaned toward the passenger seat. "How about I stop and bring us back a pizza?"

"No, I don't feel like eating." Her stomach rumbled in protest.

"Okay. How about I get myself a pizza—with double pepperoni?"

She kicked at some gravel while keeping a hand on

the doorframe. "Can you get it from Bella's? With mushrooms? And a salad."

"Anything for you. Now go inside and stay out of trouble until I get back."

She shut the door, and he slowly reversed down the driveway. She schlepped up the front porch steps and detoured to the bistro table. Her skeleton decor lay on the ground under a chair, with its top hat ripped off. *Why do I even bother?* She let it lie as it had fallen. As she stepped inside, Buddy trotted toward her from the kitchen. He placed his forepaws on her shins and flipped his tail merrily from side to side. She squatted, hugged him, and scratched under his chin.

"Hey, fur baby. I can always count on you to make me smile. TV with Dad, pizza, and you. That's all I need."

CHAPTER 18

Olivia woke up on Wednesday wishing the day would pass her by. Her alarm gently sounded, welcoming the morning with a mixed melody of field birds singing over a piano serenade. She hit snooze and drifted. Her backup chimed five minutes later, this time more matter-of-factly. She silenced the grating digital beeping by blindly tapping the screen. Ten minutes more, and her fail-safe "Mission Impossible" ring tone rudely stole her from a dream.

She reached for her phone and checked the time, lingering fondly on her lone calendar notification. She rolled over and sat on the edge of the bed, eyeing a framed photo on her dresser of her and Paige from a night two years ago in front of Ford's Theater in D.C. "Happy birthday, my friend."

After showering and dressing, she joined her father in the kitchen, where he stood by the sink, drying a cast-iron skillet with a tea towel. A glass vase brimming with a voluminous bouquet of white mini calla lilies and fresh lavender sprigs adorned the table.

"Where did those come from?" she asked.

"A delivery person from Flora's Florist Gallery brought them a few minutes ago."

"Who sent them?"

"There's a card, but I didn't look at it. I think they're meant for you. Nobody sends me flowers anymore."

She grinned and reached in, plucking out a printed card attached to a plastic holder wedged between the stems. She opened it, smiling wider as she read.

Her father nested the skillet inside a larger one resting in the storage drawer under the oven. "So, who's sending my daughter flowers?"

She set the card on the table and grabbed a mug from the cabinet. She took a deep breath, keeping her tone casual and carefree. "They're from Daniel."

He spritzed the countertop with kitchen cleaner and ripped a paper towel off the dispenser with more oomph than was necessary. "Why is he sending you flowers?"

"He texted me yesterday. He didn't know about what had happened in May. He just wanted to make sure I was okay."

"It's a little late for that, don't you think?" He stomped on the trashcan's foot lever, popping the top, and then threw the paper towel away.

"He was concerned. It was nice of him to send these. They're beautiful, don't you think?"

He looked at her and then pulled out the crossword puzzle from the newspaper's style section. He folded it in half and then in half again. "What are your plans for the day?"

"I batched several columns for my editor last week, so I don't have to do any writing. I just have an online chat for work tomorrow. I'm going into town to speak with Ellen and then return a shirt I borrowed from Sophia." Her phone rang, and she peeked at the caller ID. "It's my boss from work. I need to take this."

She stepped out of the kitchen and into the living room, where she plopped down on the sofa. "Angela, I wasn't expecting to hear from you today."

"You found a body! Why didn't you call me?"

"Good morning to you, too." Buddy pattered over to her and planted his paws on the sofa's edge. She pinned the phone between her ear and shoulder, picked him up, and settled him beside her. He laid his head on her thigh as she stroked the short, soft, black and brown fur on his back. "Why would I call you, and how do you even know? Have you finally exhausted the AP feed for fodder and are now resorting to scouring the *Apple Station Times* for filler?"

"I heard it from a friend of a friend. Give me the details. We can do something with this."

"There's nothing to tell, Angela. It's a nonstory. I'm not involved." *Of course there's a story, and I'm definitely involved.* The last thing she wanted, though, was to be the focus of any articles at her own newspaper. She had no desire for that kind of spotlight, and she shuddered at what havoc becoming a cause célèbre would bring to her inbox and social media feeds.

"Olivia, this could be a path to a whole new career for you. Investigative journalist? That has a nice ring to it. It could lead to bigger things for you. Maybe even TV spots."

She rubbed Buddy's belly. "Nope."

"I don't want you to think that I'm pressing here, but have you given any more consideration to your long-term plans? You've been living there for what, five or six months? Have you thought about when you'll be moving back? You know, they'd still take you up in New York. I had a conference with the corporate office in Manhattan last week, and people there were asking about you."

She glanced into the kitchen and lowered her voice. "I've been here five months. I'm not sure yet. Why? Is there a problem with me not being there full time? Have you heard something?"

"Hold on, let me close the door … okay. This is just between us. Word is that corporate is making cuts. Profits are slimmer, and if history is predictive—and that's not even in question, because we know in this business, it is— then staff layoffs are in the works. I don't have a handle on specifics, but I think you need to consider diversifying. You have a good track record and reputation here. Get yourself prepared. Put yourself in the best situation in case things go sideways. We'll talk more about it next week at the section meeting. You're still planning on attending, right?"

She massaged her neck. Possible cuts. There was no possible about it. In the last round of layoffs, the company had released a Pulitzer Prize winner, the managing editor, and four veteran columnists. "Yeah, I'm coming. Will you let me know if you hear anything before then?"

"Of course. Try not to worry too much about it. I've got to scoot to a meeting. Don't forget about the online chat tomorrow."

"How could I? It's my absolute, most favorite day of the entire week."

"Moan and groan all you like, but the attendance metrics are strong, especially after you developed your reputation for going off the rails."

"I do not."

"I'm not complaining. Your unpredictability when we go live is brilliant for audience engagement. With that in mind, we're shifting to a twice weekly schedule, starting next month. Okay, good talk. Gotta go. Bye."

"Angela, no. Angela? Hello?"

Buddy lifted his head and then sprung off the couch. She stared at her screen saver—a photo of her dad lifting her over a wave coming into shore when she was five. She felt as if the white water of that wave had just rolled over her. Facing potential staff cuts was only slightly more gut churning than doubling down on her streaming Q&As.

She looked at her calendar, lingering again on today's

lone entry: "Paige's birthday." She tapped open a photo album from two years ago and scrolled through pictures of her and Paige when they had attended *A Christmas Carol* at Ford's Theater in D.C. Paige had driven into town and stayed at her condo in Georgetown over that weekend. They had seen the show on Friday, gone to brunch in Old Town Alexandria on Saturday, and spent Sunday baking cookies and binging *Downton Abbey*.

She pushed up from the sofa, sauntered into the kitchen, and admired the flowers Daniel had sent. Mini callas. That was to be her bridal bouquet. Not that plans ever got that far between them. It was a throwaway line during a silly "what if" conversation they had one snowy weekend in Vermont. He never remembered anything she only ever said once. Until now. She snapped a photo of the blooms and then let the memory be. She gathered Sophia's shirt and a takeaway breakfast, and then she left for Saint Luke's cemetery.

CHAPTER 19

Olivia pulled into the parking lot of Saint Luke's Church at eleven o'clock. The historic stone building dated from the 1850s. Blocks of stark gray limestone, darkened by age, characterized the structure's enduring strength. Three windows along each side of the church popped against the drab, weathered backdrop with their bright white frames. Four recently restored concrete steps, guarded by a railing, led to the arched double entry door. She walked to the entrance and peeked inside for old times' sake. Though renovated and modernized with central air and heat, the interior retained its charming simplicity. The atrium segued into a modest, serene nave with a center aisle flanked on each side by fifteen oak pews. Weekly services were no longer held, but the assigned pastor allowed weddings and funerals with the proper parochial signatures. She had been inside for occasions of both sorts over the years, and once upon a time, even had considered it for her own nuptials.

That was all in the past, though, and today, her aim was the cemetery that occupied the surrounding church grounds. Century-old graves aligned next to those from the present day. Sometimes, she would come here and stroll among the memorial stones when she visited her mother's grave, imagining the lives of those that rested by reading how their loved ones had remembered them: "Father and Husband," "Teacher and Artist," "Adored and Cherished." One stone simply stated: "I Told You I Was Sick."

Paige's gravesite was a short distance from the parking lot, down a gently sloped section of dormant grass dotted by dogwoods and crape myrtles. June Warner was standing with her head bowed in front of Paige's memorial. Olivia slowed her pace as she walked toward her, stepping lightly so as not to disturb her from her thoughts. She stopped a few feet shy and waited as June repositioned a potted orange chrysanthemum.

June turned toward her as she dabbed her eyes with a tissue. "Olivia, a friendly face is exactly what I needed right now. I told myself I wouldn't be sad today. I'd remember the good times ... but still, it's overwhelming."

"I feel the same way," Olivia said as she stood next to June and wrapped an arm around her shoulders. "This morning I was looking at photos from a couple of years ago when Paige came to D.C. for the weekend. It seems like yesterday."

June dried her cheek. "It'll take time. After losing her father, it was hard for both of us, but at least we had each other. In the first year, you live through all the anniversaries. Like this one. The first birthday without her. Then, the first Christmas, the first Mother's Day. The second year is when the finality hits. I've learned that the grief never gets better, but you get better. We'll all get better. She would want us all to move forward. Live our lives and be happy." She ran her hand along the top of the memorial stone. "I'll let you alone to spend some time with her."

"Please, you don't have to leave," Olivia said.

"I was about to go, anyway. I'm here most days. Remember her as she would've wanted."

Olivia smiled and nodded, swallowing back tears. June touched the stone once more, and then walked toward the parking lot, leaving Olivia alone for her visit.

She stood still, allowing her eyes to well while recalling their last meeting. Paige had embraced her with an enthusiasm and glee that almost knocked her off her feet. Olivia had schemed to surprise Paige that week with her trip home to Apple Station. But Paige had trumped her with plans of her own to reveal both a budding romance and the familial secrets of A.J.'s past.

A car door shut, an engine started, and a minute later, another vehicle rolled into the lot. Crunching leaves spurred her to peek over her shoulder. She whipped her head around, shooting straight to a simmer as Preston strode toward her. *Of all places, of all days, he had to come find me here.*

She jammed her hands into her hoodie's pockets and pivoted square to him. "What are you doing here? Have you come to question me? Or is it an arrest today? I think I have a valid reason to be here. So, if you could leave me alone now, I would appreciate it." She stared off to the side, narrowing her eyes. "You let Payne put me in a cell and then you leave me in there for hours? My dad had to come get me. Were you even going to come back?" She turned in a huff to face the stone. "I get put in a cell because I'm a threat to what? To whom?"

He held his out hands with open palms. "I was just doing my—"

"Job. Yeah, got it, Detective. Loud and clear." She faced him again. "Is there anything else I can do for you? How did you know I was even here?" She wiped a flustered tear from the corner of her eye, angry more at herself for letting her emotions get the best of her. *Calm down, Liv. This isn't about him.* She paused, took a deep breath, and softened her stance. "Look, I'm sorry. It's Paige's birthday. It's been a rough morning."

The revelation was met with a nod and sympathetic eyes. "You don't have to say anything. I understand. Look, I'm sorry I had to leave yesterday. You were sleeping, and I thought that was probably the best way for you to spend your time there until Payne released you. He was trying to rattle you. He had no intention of ques-

SILENCE SAYS THE MOST

tioning you. When I called to check in, Jayden said you had already left. And for the record, I didn't know you were here. I'm not here for you."

"Oh." She looked around. "Okay." *Of course, why would you think he came here for you?*

"It's my dad." He pointed farther into the field. "He's buried about thirty yards that way. Two rows up from here and then follow straight, just to the left of the dogwood. The anniversary of his death is on Saturday. My mother and I come together every year on the day, but I always tidy up the site beforehand. Pull the weeds, clean up the stone, tend to whatever else needs tending."

She looked toward his father's site, noting the location was near to her mother's grave. The coincidence piqued her curiosity, but she let her questions be until another day, when perhaps their discussions would be more personal.

"Olivia, I'm going to say this again, even though you don't want to hear it. Whatever you were hoping to accomplish at Whispering Meadows yesterday isn't worth getting arrested over. We're working on solid leads, but I still feel there could be a threat to your safety."

She offered a quizzical smile, further easing her tone. "You're not going to assign police protection to me again, are you?"

He matched her conciliatory demeanor. "If you force my hand, I will."

She knew he wasn't bluffing, and in a heartbeat, Cole and Burt would once again be assigned to her security detail if she gave him cause. She couldn't help but to think that he would do the same for anyone else. Still, his concern seemed out of proportion to what she perceived the threat to be, but she didn't want him to worry about her.

"I was following up a lead as a favor for Ellen, but spending the afternoon in a jail cell has given me a fresh perspective on the matter. I'm being careful as you asked, watching my back and locking my doors. I have your number cued up on speed dial if my spider-sense tingles at all. I don't want any of your resources diverted to me unnecessarily. Besides, Apple Station has provided me with more excitement in the past five months than all the years I spent in D.C. combined, and I just want to live a quiet and somewhat normal life while I'm still here."

He bent forward and swept a fallen red oak leaf off the chrysanthemum. "Do you think you'll be moving back to Georgetown soon?"

She removed her hands from her pockets, running one through the lengths of her hair, grateful for the change in subject. "I'm not sure. This morning I was talking to my editor, and there are whispers of changes coming with probable staffing cuts. She strongly urged that I consider diversifying my skill set, which would mean expanding my role with the paper. This remote situation is working for now, but in the long run, I'm not sure it's sustainable. I love being here with my dad, but I don't know. My editor suggested there still may be a position for me in New York. It's a lot to mull over. What about you? Do you harbor any plans for big-time law enforcement? FBI? Some super-secret spy agency?"

He laughed, looking off to the side and then back at her. "Spy agency, huh? No. I've gotten used to life here. I have all I need. Mostly, anyway." He lifted his Stetson and ran his hand over his head. "Well, I should let you continue your visit." He tuned and paced forward a few steps but then stopped and faced her. "For what it's worth, Olivia, you'd be missed by more than just your father if you left. Stay out of the investigation. Jail cells don't suit you."

She suppressed a smile as her stomach fluttered, watching him as he turned back around and walked to his father's grave.

CHAPTER 20

Olivia drove back to town and parked near Carol's Comforts, two suites down from the newspaper's office. Normally, parking was at a premium along the busy block. The whole curb, though, from the quaint gift shop to past Daisy's Feed and Saddlery, was vacant and dotted by orange traffic cones. She slid down out of her Expedition, grabbed her phone and Sophia's shirt, and then waved to Sawyer Westin. Her longtime friend worked part time repairing tack at Daisy's when he wasn't attending to chores on his father's ranch. Today, though, he was showcasing a dark chestnut quarter horse that was tethered to a hitching post outside of the saddlery. She recognized Gypsy, the gentle mare, that he always saddled for her whenever they met for trail rides.

"Hey, Sawyer. What's Gypsy doing so far from home? Are you giving free rides on the town square now?"

His smile twinkled as they leaned in toward one

another, kissing each other on the cheek. "Nah. Gyps is here for show and tell. I'm taking her out to Fields Farm soon. They have buses coming from the elementary school, and they set up a ring for her. You know Gyps, tame as can be. The kids will be able to get up close and pet her—even sit in her saddle if they want to."

"Can they ride her?"

"If their parents are with them. We have consent forms they'd have to sign. All that legal stuff. That's not my deal. We have a few stable hands coming to keep everyone safe."

"Why is she out here?"

"Pulling double duty." He patted and rubbed along the horse's back. "Daisy has a local artist inside who's a friend of hers. She does landscape paintings, drawings, and prints. You should check out her work. It's pretty good. I brought the old girl here to help drum up some business for them. Passers-by wander over to see Gyps, and then I slide in my pitch for the showing. I've already seen two people leave carrying framed art." He reached into a brown leather treat pouch hanging from the post and pulled out a handful of carrots, offering them to the mare. "All in a day's work for you, right, Gyps?" He turned back to Olivia. "What about you? What are you up to today?"

She glanced down the sidewalk toward the newspaper's office as Ellen bolted out of the door, heading in the opposite direction. "That's why. I have to speak with Ellen. Sorry, I need to catch her. Best of luck with the showing." She patted Gypsy's side. "You be a good girl for Sawyer."

"Call me when you want to go riding again."

"Will do." She hustled down the street. "Ellen, wait up."

Ellen glanced over her shoulder and waved her on without breaking her brisk stride. "Great timing, Olivia. Walk with me. Tell me what you know."

"That's what we need to talk about. I don't know or want to know any more. I slept in a jail cell for hours yesterday."

"Cooper tells me the police only detained you. That's not what I asked you to do. You got caught doing whatever it was you were doing at Whispering Meadows. I like your spunk, though. Keep pushing. Honestly, it would've been fabulous if Payne had arrested you. Can you imagine the coverage we could've gotten on that? The headline: 'Chief of Police Arrests Hometown Hero.' That would've gone viral."

Olivia stopped as Ellen kept at her blistering pace. She raised her voice. "Ellen, I don't work for you or your paper."

Ellen turned and stepped back toward her. She grabbed Olivia's elbow and gently tugged, encouraging her to move along. "We could discuss that. I could use someone with your experience on staff. Keep walking. I'm late for a working lunch at the inn for Friday's fundraiser. I need you to stay on this. Just keep your eyes and ears open over the next couple of days until

Cassandra returns. Is that too much to ask, even if you don't work for the paper? Honestly, Olivia. Do you think Cooper is up to the task? Maybe you would've rather it had been him sitting in jail yesterday."

"Of course not. And that's a low blow. But I didn't want to be there either."

They arrived at the inn, and Ellen opened one of the double French doors, ushering Olivia onward. "If you don't want to finish what you've started, that's fine. I'll find someone else."

The comforting aromatic air of slow-cooked, country cuisine instantly soothed Olivia as she stepped into the lobby. Since moving back, she and her father had frequently dined here at the invitation of the owner, Bev.

Halloween was prime booking time for the historic boutique inn. Preston's mother aggressively advertised it as a premier destination for those wanting a true haunting experience, thanks to an unsolved murder on the second floor dating back to the early 1900s. Bev had spared no details in decorating the lobby for the season. Fake cobwebs suspending 3D paper spiders draped along the walls, and flickering, flameless votive candles lit jack-o'-lanterns lined the welcome counter. The pièce de résistance was a life-sized plastic skeleton posed sitting on a chair behind the reception desk, leaning on its elbows.

Bev scuttled out of the dining room with her arms extended, brushing by Ellen and embracing Olivia with a hearty hug. "My dear, how wonderful that you'll be joining our small but mighty committee for the fundraiser."

"Oh, no. I was just walking this way with Ellen." She tried to wiggle out of Bev's robust snare, but remained within her hold, awkwardly suspending her in a half-hug. She offered Bev one more light squeeze and then forcefully broke free.

Jenn and Chris entered the lobby from the dining room, swinging their entwined hands like lovesick teens. "Hi, Olivia," Jenn said, as her cherry cheeks popped with genuine delight.

"Aren't these two the most adorable couple?" Bev said.

Jenn's smile beamed even brighter. "We're here checking out the banquet room and menu options for our wedding rehearsal dinner."

"Oh yes, we're very popular with weddings," Bev said. "We made the top ten list for small-town southern wedding venues as named by *Brides to Be* magazine." She winked at Olivia. "I'm sure when you're ready to get married, this will be a fine place to host your reception, or perhaps even the wedding itself."

Ellen stepped toward the dining room. "Bev, I'm going to join the others. Olivia, we'll talk later."

"Ellen, wait," Olivia protested. "We're not done here." But they were. Ellen was already gone, and whatever Olivia had planned to accomplish had failed miserably. She politely smiled at the eye-gazing couple. "So, do you think you'll be hosting your rehearsal dinner here?"

"I do," Jenn said.

Chris enfolded her hand as if she was a fairytale princess and brushed her fingers with a gallant, gentle kiss. "And I do, too, forever and a day, love you."

Jenn giggled, and Olivia felt like she was an extra in a Hallmark movie.

"We had planned to use the ballroom at Whispering Meadows, but we decided the inn would suit us better," Jenn said.

"Bev would love to have you here," Olivia replied. "The food is fabulous, and the ambiance couldn't be more romantic."

A three-and-a-half-foot tall flash sporting a red hoodie darted from the dining room. Mikey ran up to Olivia and hit the brakes, staring at the phone in her hand.

"Mikey, get back here," Melissa said as she hurried after him.

He snatched Olivia's phone from her loose hold.

"Mikey, give it back to her." Melissa wrested the cell from his fingers and returned it to Olivia. "I'm sorry. I thought I could bring him here while we held our meeting, but it's been one of those mornings. His routine is all messed up now."

He squatted and ran his hand along the carpeted floor.

"Mikey, that's dirty. I need to get him out of here. I promised him we would visit the farm when we were done with lunch." She kneeled on one knee and zipped up his hoodie. "Are you ready to go down the big slides and pick a pumpkin?"

Bev stepped toward the lobby counter. "If you're going out to Fields Farm, I have a coupon here to save you on the admission." She gingerly lifted the skeleton's arm and slipped a discount voucher from a small stack under the bony fingers.

"Thank you, Bev. Call me if we need to meet again tomorrow. Come on, Mikey." She grasped Mikey's hand, and they left the inn.

Chris checked his watch. "We need to be going, too. I have a scheduled call with our attorney in thirty minutes. We're finalizing the details on the sale of the farm."

"Are the buyers local, or can't you say yet?" Olivia asked.

"It's no secret. Crescent Valley Organics. They're based in the Midwest. They're an up-and-coming mid-sized company that wants to expand their operations and distribution to the southeast and mid-Atlantic."

"And your parents have decided not to sell any of their property to Philip Wayne?"

Chris softened his shoulders. "I must apologize for my behavior yesterday at the country club. It's just that I wouldn't put it past him to jeopardize the sale. He's been wanting that acreage by his winery because it's next to his vineyards. Having that land would easily triple, maybe even quadruple, his production. But my parents never wanted to sell the property in parcels."

"You believe, though, that Whispering Meadows is responsible for the algae bloom at the lake," Olivia said.

"I know it is," he replied.

Jen shook her head. "Chris, we don't know that. You can't go around accusing him based on your history. I went to the lake this morning to take pictures to send to the VDEQ. I figured, considering what all has happened, it could be days before they dispatch someone else, and I wanted to make sure the bloom wasn't getting worse. Something like that can get out of hand quickly and damage the ecosystem in a short time. Besides that, if it was worsening, the park would need to be temporarily closed for the community's safety. But, from what I saw, the bloom is already dissipating."

Chris checked his watch again. "I'm sorry. I really need to be going."

"Of course," Olivia said. "It was good to see you both. Congratulations on your choice of venue here. I know Bev will make it a night to remember."

Chris and Jen left after exchanging parting pleasantries. Bev grabbed Olivia's hand and offered a loving squeeze. "I hope you remember that as well. Are you sure I can't convince you to join our committee?"

"I'm sorry. I have some work to do."

"Okay. Why don't you come this weekend with your father for dinner? I'll invite Preston. Seven o'clock on Saturday. It's a date." She wrapped Olivia in a smothering hug and then strode back into the dining room before she could think of a thing to say.

She stood alone in the lobby with Sophia's shirt in hand. *Apparently, I'm covering a murder for a paper I don't work for, have been set up again for a dinner date by a matchmaking mother, and I need a plus one—who doesn't exist—for a wine tasting.* She paced to the counter and leaned over, lifting the skeleton's wrist to swipe a coupon off the stack. "Believe me, Bones, I know exactly how you feel."

CHAPTER 21

With the coupon and Sophia's shirt in hand, Olivia left the inn. The orange traffic cones that had blocked the street now sat stacked on the sidewalk. Sawyer's truck and an attached single horse trailer were parked in front of Daisy's. A small group of pedestrians had gathered and were watching as Sawyer walked beside Gypsy, gently coaxing her into the transport.

Olivia crossed the town square, beelining for the clinic. It was a typical weekday afternoon, with townsfolk coming or going, hustling or moseying, depending on their purpose. A landscaping crew was spreading mulch to-and-fro about the fall flower beds that adorned the gazebo. Laborers toting buzzing blowers shooed leaves into tidy piles for riding vacuum mowers to clear. The benches served as meeting spots for those eating lunch or chatting with friends. She spied the Peabodys by the little library. Floyd selected a book, and then Dorothy handed him one from her purse to put in.

She entered Sophia's clinic, setting off a welcome chime. Tori, who was sitting on the foyer's sofa, glanced up from her phone and tsk-tsked her with a sigh. "Hey there, jailbird."

Olivia threw Sophia's shirt onto the sofa and then turned to leave. "Tell Soph I said thanks. I'm out of here."

Tori popped up from the couch and wrapped an arm around her shoulders to one-eighty her stride. "Wait. Come back. I'm teasing you. Tell her yourself. Don't leave."

Tyler crawled over from the children's play area. He grabbed Olivia's pants and then pulled himself into standing. He bounced a few times, let go, and fell. Tori scooped him up, settled him on the round carpet in the corner, and dumped a container of large building blocks by his feet.

"Mommy wants you to build her a tall tower." She stepped back toward Olivia and lowered her voice. "Okay. Let's hear it. Tell me everything."

Olivia sat, resting her head against the sofa's high back. "Hear what?"

Tori crossed her arms like a schoolmarm. "Don't give me that, dear. You got thrown in the slammer. That's serious street cred. Did you get a tattoo? I bet you started a book club on your cell block. I hear that's a thing."

She rolled her head to one side. "I hardly think that the time-out sin bin at the station qualifies as a slammer."

Sophia strolled out of the treatment gym as red and green building blocks landed by Olivia's feet. She picked up Sophia's shirt. "I brought this back. It's clean. I was trying to explain to our friend here that yesterday's incident was a misunderstanding."

"How come Soph hears about it last night, but I'm relegated to the day-old bread rack?" Tori said.

Olivia stared at the ceiling. "Is that a serious question?"

Tyler giggled and launched a volley of blocks over his head. Sophia gathered them together and placed them on the stove of the play kitchenette.

"Time to dish," Sophia said. "You wrote in your text last night that you'd explain more today. It's now today, so what were you really doing at the country club?"

Olivia folded her hands in her lap, casual as could be. "I'm considering taking up golf. I met someone who gives private lessons. Rhett. He's a pro."

A plastic egg and a faux corncob were either being served or no longer needed by Tyler in the play corner.

Sophia and Tori eyed each other. "Really?" Tori said. "You were just minding your own business, and Preston decides on a whim to detain you because you want to putt around with Rhett?"

"Not exactly."

Tori raised her eyebrows. "Did he handcuff you?"

"Don't even start. I wasn't arrested."

A phone rang from an office in the hallway, and Sophia backpedaled, pointing at Olivia. "Don't you skip out on me."

Tori stepped over to the play corner and swooped Tyler up in her arms. "Ready to go? It's snack time for you. We've got to make sure you're big and strong, and then maybe you, too, can be a police detective someday." She turned back to Olivia with a mischievous smile. "What's with you two, anyway?"

She shrugged her shoulders. "Who's us two?"

"Don't insult me, Liv. You're single, and Preston's quite handsomely single."

She scooted to the edge of the sofa and gave Tyler a high five. "I think I'm going to leave. It's my snack time, too."

"That's exactly what I thought. Your silence says everything. Wave bye-bye to Auntie Liv, Ty-Ty. Don't mind her, though; she's a bit tongue-tied today. Maybe her new friend Rhett could help her with that."

Tyler waved and grabbed Olivia's hair, playfully lifting it and blowing raspberries.

"Let go of Auntie." Tori unclenched his fingers and then carried him out of the clinic.

Olivia slumped back down on the couch and refolded Sophia's shirt. She dug her phone out of her pocket and scrolled through her messages while she was waiting. The most recent were the brief texts she had exchanged with Sophia from last night. Below them was the one from Daniel she still had not answered.

The flowers he had sent were her favorites, and though she ascribed no meaning to the gesture, she had, at least, softened around his memory. She opened a browser on her phone and searched for his new firm in California.

It wouldn't have worked long term between them. She wasn't the west coast kind, and she never would've moved that far from her father. She wouldn't, though, allow Daniel to use her as an excuse for holding him back. Besides, she had her life to live. A life in which she ran her own agenda, rather than everyone else's, for a change.

She looked at the company directory, scrolling through the headshots and bios of the associates. There he was, wearing the burgundy striped tie she had given him for luck and beaming the same captivating smile that had charmed so many of her days and nights.

She stood and walked over to the table by the window, peering across the town square at the inn. Chris and Jenn, now there was a perfect couple. Practically made for each other. She was happy for them and even happier that Bev would have a rehearsal dinner to host. She pulled out a chair and sat, glancing down the hallway and hearing Sophia still dealing with the details of a delivery.

She flipped through a math workbook Maria had left on the table from one of her tutoring sessions. Mathematics for first graders. The module's objectives: counting to 120, understanding addition and subtraction as the reverse of each other, putting two shapes together to form a new one and then dividing it into parts. The first lesson put her to the test. Paul has three chickens, Peter has six cows, and Mary has four lambs. How many animals do they have altogether?

E-I-E-I-O. She paused, thinking of a toy barn she had played with as a child. The set had livestock animals of all shapes and sizes, and an optional silo that offered expansion for the make-believe farming operation.

Bingo. She opened a new tab on her phone's browser and searched for Crescent Valley Organics. It was a larger company than Chris had led her to believe. Though headquartered in Wisconsin, they had corporate offices in California and Northern Europe as well.

She searched again, this time for news of the Fields Farm acquisition. An article from an organic agricultural trade media site ranked first. The impetus for the farm's purchase was to expand the company's presence along the Atlantic coast with closer distribution to the north-eastern markets. The piece stated further that the purchase would be a win after a failed attempt to acquire a larger operation in North Carolina. The sellers, in that case, had backed out of the deal over pending litigation involving charges of unlawful termination brought on by a former Crescent Valley employee.

She entered the search terms: Crescent Valley Organics, lawsuit, and unlawful termination. Three articles popped up, all of which rehashed the facts from the first ones that she had read. She added "settlement" to the query and spied the headline: "Court Rules in Favor of Whistleblower."

She tapped the link and skimmed the opening paragraph to the bottom line: "The court dismissed the case as Crescent Valley Organics settled with Jason Rotterdam for an undisclosed amount." She hit the read more button quicker than the beat of a hummingbird's wings and ran straight into a paywall. She sidestepped and shimmied by the blockade, entering enough keywords to get the protected article to show on a completely random law review journal page.

Jason had been a researcher in the company's emerging technology division, and he had accused his employer of misrepresenting results of internal studies involving the efficacy of a new organic pesticide. The motive, he claimed, was to stabilize capital investment in the company and buttress flagging profits for shareholders. The company, in turn, accused Jason of stealing intellectual property and intending to sell the research to a rival competitor.

A popcorn kernel bounced off Olivia's cheek. She side-glanced at Sophia, standing beside her with a snack bowl in hand.

"I've been here for like a literal hour," Sophia said. "Did you not hear me?"

Olivia picked the popcorn off her shirt and tossed it into her mouth. "Listen to this. Jason Rotterdam, aka creepy squirrel hunter from the lake, used to work for

Crescent Valley Organics. The same company that's about to buy Fields Farm."

Sophia leaned against the table, extending the Talavera bowl toward Olivia. "Okay. Admittedly, that's a weird coincidence."

She pushed her chair back, stood, and grabbed a handful of popcorn. "Or not. He was a researcher working on emerging technologies. Specifically, a new organic pesticide."

The front door chimed as a boy wearing a superhero cape entered using a walker, followed by his mother, who held the door open for him.

"Hey, Brooks," Sophia said. "Go right in. I'll be there in a second. I hope you brought your jumping legs with you today."

The young boy and his mother passed through the lobby, and then Olivia stepped toward the entrance. "Have fun."

"Hey, where are you going?"

She paused with her hand on the knob. "Don't you find that curious? The bloom? Jason lives right there. He worked for the same company that's buying the farm."

"I don't like where this is heading. Drop it. You've already used up one of your nine lives. Need I remind you about the last time, when you—"

"This isn't like that. That was about Paige and A.J."

"Exactly. What's this to you? Why are you even pursuing this? And don't give me that line about this being a favor for Ellen."

The picture Mikey had drawn flashed in her mind. Preston was right. She was involved somehow. Mikey was saying something, and although she didn't feel threatened, she wasn't about to let her guard down. She shrugged her shoulders, painting on an innocent grin. "Who knows? Maybe I'll reinvent myself as an investigative journalist. Digging deep, solving crimes, tackling cold cases."

"That's not funny. I've got clients waiting. Could you try to be a little more normal?"

Olivia polished off her popcorn and then offered a salute that Sam would be proud of. "Roger that."

"Where are you going?"

She cracked the door. "It's such a nice day. I think I'll visit Fields Farm and enjoy the fall festival activities in my attempt to be a little more normal. I've got a coupon. By the way, Cole has been asking about you."

Sophia dismissed her, waving her hand with disgust. "Don't even bring that up. You still owe me big time for indulging that blind date. And don't call me to bail you out of jail."

CHAPTER 22

On weekends from mid-September until after Halloween, cars and SUVs from near and far jammed the parking lot for Fields Farm. Within an hour's drive, there were four other family farms hosting similar fall festivals, and Olivia had been to all of them many times over the years.

Pumpkin patches, corn mazes, and hayrides were all standard fare. Petting barns, pig races, and pumpkin chucking were specialty draws that lured families from farm to farm throughout the autumnal season. Early, eager visitors raided the pumpkin patches, selecting the plumpest of the crop to carve into cute or creepy jack-o'-lanterns. Each farm had a signature draw. Tidewells had the best jams, fruit butters, and pies. Rolling Hills was a favorite with children. Where else could a kid fire a corn cannon, ride a pedal car, and plunge down a country coaster all in the same hour?

Fields Farm's claim to fame was apple cider donuts, and that was no small thing. A TV episode of *Best of Southern Fried* had once featured the specialty, galvanizing local pride and acclaim. On festival weekends, lines formed quickly in the marketplace barn whenever a farmhand rang the bell to signal a fresh batch had been boxed and was ready for sale.

The parking lot was little more than a cordoned-off half acre of ground worn bare and deeply rutted by attendees of the various seasonal festivals throughout the year. On busy weekends, vehicles aligned in tightly packed, jaunty rows. But at two o'clock on a Wednesday, the field was wide open, with only a few dozen cars and three school buses to maneuver around.

Olivia drove cautiously over the pocked and furrowed ground. Her Expedition bounced and jostled as her tires dipped in craters deep enough to stress the struts of smaller cars. She pulled up to the front row and parked near the admission tent, where a farmhand was sitting and painting a pumpkin at a folding table. The marketplace barn was a short walk up a slight slope from the entrance gate. Beyond the barn, a cheerful sunflower field radiated in full bloom. She had wandered among these giants in the past, marveling at the stalks that stood as tall as her and delighting in the blossoms that were larger than her hands.

As she was paying for her admission, gleeful screaming erupted by the entrance to the corn maze. Cooper was standing by the start, high fiving a group of spirited kiddos. He handed an orange flag with a number on it to a chaperone, and then the eager team entered the labyrinth. Melissa was there too, speaking on her phone while Mikey tugged on her arm, trying to break free.

Olivia waved and walked over to Cooper. "Hey, Cooper. What are you doing here?"

"Mrs. Fields enlisted me as a backup corn cop."

"Excuse me?"

He pointed to a gold badge resembling an ear of corn with a cowboy hat that was pinned to his Washington Nationals sweatshirt. "I'm Sheriff Cobb for the next two hours. Mrs. Fields needed extra hands today with the busloads of kids from the elementary school. Her regular day-shifter is repairing a tractor in the equipment barn. She called for reinforcements, and here I am—designated rescuer." He stepped to his side and tapped a wooden, hand-painted sign next to a set of steps leading to an observation platform. "Everyone who enters gets a flag with a number on it. If you get lost or need help, you can text an SOS to 800-WAYWARD, wave your flag, and we'll send in a posse for the rescue."

"Mikey, stand still. I'm sorry, ma'am, can you give me a second. I'm with my son here," Melissa said, speaking on her phone.

Olivia glanced at Melissa as Mikey was rocking from side to side. She turned back toward Cooper. "Have you ever had to rescue anyone?"

"Why? What have you heard? If you're talking about

Mrs. Penny's grandson, we were playing hide and seek. He wasn't officially lost."

Mikey bolted from Melissa's side, heading straight for the entrance to the maze. Olivia shuffled to block him and then gently placed her hands on his shoulders. "Whoa there, little buddy. I think you're forgetting your mommy."

Melissa jogged over with her phone pressed to her ear. "Please, hold on for just another minute." She lowered her cell and grabbed Mikey's hand while looking at Olivia. "Hi, again. Sorry. Thanks for catching him. Come on, Mikey."

He pulled against her, slipping an arm out of his jacket's sleeve. She pinned the phone between her shoulder and ear and lowered her voice. "Mikey, stop. Now." She maneuvered his arm back into his sleeve and zipped up the hoodie.

Olivia squatted and pulled her phone out of her pocket. "I can take him through the maze if that's okay with you. I don't mind at all."

Melissa shook her head. "No. Thanks, though."

"I'd be happy to." She gestured toward Melissa's cell. "It seems like you have your hands full. Cooper, how long does it take to get through? Fifteen, twenty minutes?"

He shrugged, pursing his lips. "I've never made it through the whole way by myself."

Olivia opened a music app and searched for a children's playlist. She stood, hit the top of the feed, and showed Mikey the screen. He stilled, watching visual patterns dance to the music's beat. "I'm pretty sure we'll be okay, as long as I have a signal. And I have close personal ties with Sheriff Cobb here if we need a rescue."

"Um … okay. Thank you," Melissa said. She lowered her phone and leaned down, tipping his chin to align her face with his as he turned slightly away. "Mikey, you go with Ms. Olivia. Listen to her."

Olivia clasped his hand. "Come on, Mikey. Let's go explore the maze."

Melissa stepped a few feet away and returned to her call. "Hi. Sorry. Thank you for your patience. You were saying …"

Cooper picked an orange flag out of a wooden whiskey barrel and pointed to the rescue hotline. "Text Sheriff Cobb if you need help."

She smiled, refusing the flag. "This isn't my first corn maze. I have my hands full, anyway. Thanks, Cooper. As always, you're my hero."

He tipped an imaginary ten-gallon hat. "Ah shucks, ma'am. Now you be careful in there. Be on the lookout for varmints."

CHAPTER 23

The maze started simply enough, as the generously wide, hard-packed trail led only one way. A mosaic of green and bone-dry stalks stood tall, obscuring alternate paths and hiding any clues to help her navigate. Remnants of brittle, papery husks and ears of golden kernel corn lay scattered along the ground. Children's voices on a path parallel to theirs debated on which way their merry band of maze runners should go.

Olivia came to her first decision as the trail bifurcated. Left or right? Four children zoomed past her, veering left as a harried adult hustled after them. She squeezed Mikey's hand tighter and went right. "Let's hope we don't have to call in the cavalry to get out of here."

They soon arrived at another fork, this one posing three paths. She glanced behind, trying to map her route, but then abandoned the plan as all the dried corn stalks looked the same. She chose right again and led Mikey straight into a dead end. She retraced her line, taking two lefts, and successfully walked in a circle. *Brilliant, Liv.*

Mikey seemed not to mind as he strolled calmly and cooperatively by her side. "Why do corn mazes always sound fun until you're actually in one?" she said, mostly to herself.

The music stopped, and he crossed in front of her, swatting at her cell. "Hold on. I'll restart it." She let go of his hand, and he took off, dashing down the path and disappearing around the nearby corner.

"Wait! Mikey, stop!" She rushed forward just a few steps behind, rounded the turn, and almost barreled into him. Mikey was standing still just around the bend, staring up at Chris, who had a long-handled shovel in hand. She grabbed Mikey's shoulders and pulled him back two steps. "Gotcha, speedster." She grasped his forearm and politely smiled at Chris. "Thanks for putting up the blockade."

He waved at Mikey. "You've got yourself a runner."

She nodded. "He's quick. That's for sure. I let go of him just for a second, and he was off."

Mikey swayed and squirmed from her light hold. She lowered to a knee and corralled him in close. She opened a video player on her phone, searched for cartoons, and hit the top of the feed. As the music started, she handed her cell to Mikey and then glanced up at Chris. "Are you one of Sheriff Cobb's deputies?"

His eyes sparked as he grinned. "Not today. Although, I've had to make my share of rescues in here."

"I can see that. It's not as easy as it looks. I've already run into a dead end and circled back on myself once. You could earn a king's ransom if you sold bags of breadcrumbs by the entrance."

Chris rested the shovel's blade on the ground. "A missed business opportunity, no doubt. Everyone gets turned around in here. It's meant to be challenging. We use designing software and GPS mapping to ensure we have plenty of misdirection and dead ends. I can let you in on a little secret." He held his hand alongside his mouth. "If you go straight down the path I just came from, look for a hidden trail on the right. It's not part of the design, but it's a shortcut I blazed, so I don't have to navigate this entire blooming thing every time something needs fixing in here."

"I'm forever in your debt. I thought I would be in here twenty minutes tops, but my corn sense must be rusty. Your secret is safe with me."

He lifted his shovel and tapped its tip into the ground several times. "My mother received reports of large ruts in the trail along the north side. As soon as my meeting was over, I came here to fill them up and tamp them down. With all these kids here today, I don't want anyone getting tripped up."

"You're a man of many talents. Negotiating the farm's sale and tending to the trail. Your parents are lucky to have you here. Does Kevin help during the festival season, too?"

"Sometimes. He's busy with his own life, though. He loves the farm, don't get me wrong. He doesn't want my parents to sell it."

"Did you two ever think about running the farm together?" She glanced down at Mikey, checking to ensure he wasn't inadvertently sending texts or posting random letters and numbers as comments on her social feeds. He remained mesmerized by the video, holding her phone inches from his face. She stood, keeping a hand on his shoulder.

"Me and Kevin? No. It would be tempting if Jenn and I were staying here in Virginia. But after the wedding, we're moving to the Netherlands."

"Wow. That's exciting. And far. And unusual."

He nodded. "It is. All of those. Jenn has a professor-ship waiting for her at one of the top universities in the world for agricultural sciences. She'll be both teaching and researching. It's her dream job. This is a once-in-a-lifetime opportunity for her. Although we love it here, we're making the leap. As for Kevin, running a place like this without the ongoing support of my parents would be too much for him."

"What do you mean?" she asked.

"I take it you don't know about Kevin. Bev told us this morning that you just moved back recently. Is that right?"

"Not exactly moved back. I think. I'm sorry. I don't

really know anything about your brother. I had never met him prior to Monday."

He rested his hands on the shovel handle. "Kevin is an army vet. He was a Ranger. That's all he ever wanted to be. The first chance he got, he enlisted and went to Ranger School. He was stationed at Fort Benning for a while, and then he did two tours in Afghanistan. During the second tour, his squad was ambushed on a routine patrol, and three of his friends were killed. Kevin took a bullet to his leg and suffered a head injury. He received treatment first in Germany, and then, when he was stable, the army transferred him to Walter Reed. He rehabbed several months up there in Bethesda, primarily for his brain injury. When the hospital released him, he lived with my parents on the farm until he could get back on his feet."

She lowered her gaze. "I'm sorry. I didn't know. It's none of my business."

"It's okay. It's old news. I think sometimes practically the entire town knows him. It was a big deal in the media when he came home. The injured war hero had returned. He had a rough time, though, adjusting to what we would consider a normal life. My dad had him working on the farm, mostly physical labor, to start. Kevin liked that. But then my dad tried to involve him in the business affairs. You can't run an operation this size by riding a tractor all day. My dad took it slow, but Kevin couldn't adjust. I know it's partially the brain injury. There are too many decisions, too much stress, too much to juggle in managing an operation like this." He leaned down to his side, picked up a dried ear of corn from the trail's edge, and flipped it into the stalks. "After watching three of your buddies die, it's hard to care about something like a corn maze."

A group of frenzied children scampered around the corner, and they shuffled to the side as the pack passed by. The cartoon ended and Mikey repeatedly tapped the screen, playing a random video on manifesting your dreams. She tilted the phone toward her and restarted the cartoon. He squatted, contented, watching dancing bears do-si-do to the lively tempo of cats fiddling a hoedown.

"Kevin's a good guy," Chris said. "Sometimes too much stress builds up, and it gets to him."

"Even though I don't know him that well, he seems suited for what he's doing now."

Chris nodded. "He is, and he loves it. Working in the parks keeps him outside. It's a lot of physical labor, and that's what he enjoys. He doesn't have to deal with many people or politics. Bev's son is the one who got him involved in the park ranger program. He's keeping his life together, and I'm proud of him. So are my parents. He's receiving a quarter-share of the sale, and that will provide him financial stability for now. I'll be getting the same. I asked my parents to give him some of my share, or at least, to keep what they had planned to give me until later in case he needed it. Jenn and I are fortunate, but Kevin may need help in the future."

Mikey stood and rocked back and forth while swiping his finger across the screen.

Why would he need help? She pressed further, tiptoeing well past her business. "I saw him at Melissa's yesterday," she said. "He almost got into a fight with Jason Rotterdam. Do you know Jason? Do they have a history together?"

"I don't know Jason personally. Kevin has told me a little about him. From what I gather, he's a troublemaker who lives out by Lake Crystal." Chris tamped down some loose ground on the side of the trail. "But that's Kevin for you. Really, my brother is harmless. Just maybe a little hotheaded sometimes."

No kidding. "And that's not a problem in his position? Isn't grace under pressure paramount to public safety?"

"Let me rephrase that. He's hotheaded mostly toward me."

Ouch. She had gone too far and overstepped her bounds. "I'm sorry. I thought … it seemed that you two got along well."

"We do. Usually. We are brothers, after all, so we've had our rivalries the same as any other siblings. At the end of the day, we have each other's backs. It's just with the wedding coming up …" He eyed the ground, turning the shovel round and round.

"I see," she said, having no clue what he meant.

He lifted his shovel and held it near the blade. "I guess you don't know about that either. Before my brother went on his second tour, the one in which he got injured, he and Jenn were engaged."

The cartoon ended, and Mikey dropped her phone on the ground. He screamed and dashed past Chris toward the opposite end of the trail.

"Wait!" she yelled. She snatched her cell, glanced at Chris, and took off after Mikey.

CHAPTER 24

Olivia caught up to Mikey before he reached the split at the end of the trail. She grabbed his hand and slowed his steps until he came to a sure-footed stop. She glanced behind, but the path was clear, as Chris had already walked away. "Come on, Mikey. Let's get out of here."

The secret shortcut Chris had shared was plain to find. The hidden path would've been easy to miss or dismiss had she not known exactly what to look for. The narrow trail was bumpy and covered by uncut corn stalks that Olivia brushed aside as they walked in single file. She led the way, keeping Mikey close and subtly tugging him forward whenever he fell behind. Louder laughter and spirited banter hinted at daylight a few feet ahead.

They emerged from the camouflaged trail twenty yards from the corn maze's official end, where Melissa was waiting while watching a group of children whooping and hollering at conquering the labyrinth.

Mikey screamed, and Melissa peered their way. She paced backward a few steps, appearing puzzled by their unexpected emergence. She waved and walked toward them. "Where did you come from? Is there more than one exit?"

Olivia released Mikey's hand but stayed close by his side. "No. We were the beneficiaries of insider information."

Melissa leaned down and kissed his cheek. "Did you have fun?" She looked up at Olivia. "Was he okay? Did he cause you any problems?"

"None at all. I think I should've let him lead."

Melissa stood tall and smoothed his hair. "Thank you for taking him. I was trying to straighten something out with the bank. I had been on hold forever, so when I reached an actual person, I didn't want to call back and start over, working through all the menus again."

"Say no more. I can relate. I'm glad I could help."

Melissa clasped Mikey's hand. "Okay, buddy. Are you ready to go to the pumpkin patch?"

They exchanged goodbyes and went their separate ways.

Olivia ducked into the marketplace barn, bought two dozen apple cider donuts, and then headed back to her car. She set the white cardboard boxes on the passenger seat, started the engine, and plugged her phone into its charger. Then she leaned her elbow on the windowsill and rested her head in her hand. The sun was setting, and the farm would soon be closed for the day. She had come here wanting to scope out the lay of the land, but what she had learned in the maze from Chris seemed far more relevant. How so, though, she wasn't sure.

The seductive smell of the freshly made donuts reminded her she hadn't eaten since her to-go breakfast on the way to the cemetery. She glanced at the dash clock and then flipped open the closest box. "Four thirty. Snack time."

She greedily grabbed a donut from one of the twin rows of six. The palm-sized treat was pillowy soft and aromatically sweet. The first bite melted in her mouth, as if the still-warm, fluffy pastry was little more than whipped air. Clean, crisp apple cider with a kiss of cinnamon tickled her taste buds and lusciously lingered. Each of her bites was larger than the last, and within a minute, she had downed the whole donut.

She wiped her hands together and then brushed them on her pants for good measure. She picked up her phone, opened a browser, and searched for details about Kevin's return to town after his injury. The article that drew her attention had been written by Paige for the *Apple Station Times*. The piece recounted the same history she had learned from Chris in the maze. There was no mention of his prior engagement to Jenn, but she knew Paige never would've exploited that angle, anyway. Olivia, herself, still didn't know what to make of it. It was certainly odd, but whether it was something or nothing remained in question.

She stared through the passenger side window at the

merchant barn and then at the sunflower field bathed in the golden-hour light. She opened her photos and revisited the picture she had snapped of Daniel's lily and lavender bouquet. It had niggled at her all day that she hadn't acknowledged receiving them, but she hadn't been sure what to say.

She reread his last text, thought a moment, and wrote a reply: "Thanks for the flowers. They're lovely. You remembered. I'm okay." She hit send and then exhaled as if she had defused a bomb. *That wasn't so hard, was it?*

As she laid the cell in the center cubby, three dots appeared under her message. She watched with bated breath and cursed her heart for ramping in her chest. Her phone rang to the tune of "Girls Just Want to Have Fun." She declined Sophia's call and then read his reply: "Of course. How could I forget?"

She smiled from a memory of a dance together in a field of French lavender under a glowing orange summer sunset sky. Then she texted back: "I'll call you next week."

He responded in a beat and was to the point: "Can't wait. Still love you."

That wasn't what she was expecting. Her phone rang again. She took a deep breath, straining for an even tone. "Hey, Soph. What's up?"

"Did you decline my call?"

"I … ah … was just … I was going to call you right back."

"Are you okay? You sound stressed."

She massaged the back of her neck. "No. I'm fine. What's going on?"

"I wanted to check in on you. You left in a hurry. I swear I need to put a tracker on you. Did you know microchipping people is a thing in Sweden?"

"That's a hard pass. I'm all in for Swedish meatballs and bookcases from IKEA, but geotracking is a bridge too far."

"So, you're okay, then?"

"Yeah. I'm at Fields Farm, but I'm about to leave." She opened the donut box and grabbed another, more out of stress than hunger. She bit off a third of her second helping and continued as she chewed. "I found out something interesting, though."

Sophia grunted and sighed. "Save it. Stop by the clinic and tell me then. A.J. is here installing a platform swing in the play gym. We're having dinner tonight if you want to stay. We should be ready around five thirty. You said you're still at the farm?"

She took another bite, wiping her mouth with the back of her hand. "Yes. I'm leaving as soon as I'm done reporting all my comings and goings to you."

"Can you bring me some of their apple cider donuts? I mean, since you're out there."

She looked and lusted at the second box. It was for the best. Really. She didn't absolutely need two dozen. She wanted them, but she accepted it as fate. "I've already gotcha covered."

She also didn't need to receive a text like that from

Daniel. Not today. All these months, she had thought that door was shut. She reread his message. *What's that supposed to mean?*

"Hello? Are you still there, Liv?"

"Sorry. What time is dinner?"

"I just said. Five thirty. Are you sure you're okay? You sound off."

She began a reply to his text. "Yeah. I'm fine. I'll come by, but I don't know about supper. I'm on my second donut now, and I'm pretty sure I'm about to have a third."

Sophia started talking about someone somewhere doing something. Olivia continued typing her text, one ear listening for any inflections or pauses that signaled it was her turn to speak. She reread what she wrote and then set the phone on the center console.

"Are you even listening to me?" Sophia asked.

"Of course. I'm on my way. I'll be there soon."

They ended the call, and she stared out the windshield for another five minutes, leaning her head against the seat. She watched as the last wagon ride for the day departed for the pumpkin patch. Within an hour, the farm would be closed, and the preparations for Thursday's festival activities would begin. *How could he say that now?* She reread her text and then backspaced over everything she had written. She tossed the phone onto the passenger seat, pulled out of the parking lot, and drove back to town in silence.

CHAPTER 25

Olivia entered the clinic with a box of apple cider donuts in hand and greeted Sophia and A.J., who were lounging on the foyer's sofa, chatting. A.J. sprung up, wrapped her in a hug, and then snatched the specialty treats from her.

"Those are for Sophia," Olivia said.

He lifted the lid, pilfering a pair. "Aha. How've you been?"

"I'm fine. Why does everyone keep asking me that?"

He set the box beside Sophia and then raised his hands, surrendering his concern. "Hold your friendly fire, Annie Oakley. It sounds like someone's hangry. You should have a donut." He extended his arm, offering his second serving. "I'm only asking, Liv, because I care. You found a freaking dead body. That's no picnic."

She declined spiking her blood sugar any further. "Oh, I'm sorry. It's not that."

"Then what is it?" Sophia asked. "Did something

happen while you were at the farm? You seemed distracted when I talked to you."

She winced, focusing on the swirls of the mosaic carpet surrounding her feet. "Daniel texted me."

"About what?" Sophia said.

A.J. settled back on the sofa. "Yeah, what does he want?"

"He wants to talk."

Sophia scowled, adding a hearty harrumph for emphasis. "He's got some nerve. Now, after all this time, he wants to talk? Did you answer him?"

"He sent flowers, too. I replied that I'd call him next week."

"Why would you do that?" A.J. said. "What could you possibly want to say to him, other than to tell him off?"

"You know things didn't go down like that between us. Our split was more about our jobs than anything else. I don't regret it. I'd make the same decision again under the circumstances. He somehow just learned about what happened in the spring. He was concerned. That's all. I still consider him a friend."

Sophia folded her arms. "Is that so?"

"Yes, that's so. Let's drop it, please. He's a nonfactor now." She playfully kicked the steel toe of A.J.'s boot. "You said that you've done work at Whispering Meadows. Have you ever spent time there besides doing that job in September?"

He grimaced, massaging the back of his neck. "Soph,

can you help me out? I just got this sudden, sharp pain. It must be the whiplash from the whirlwind change in topic."

Olivia kicked his boot again, this time a little more forcefully. "Moron."

He opened the donut box again, but Sophia slapped his hand away. "Hmm," he said. "Whispering Meadows? Sure. Every Saturday, I throw my custom golf clubs into the trunk of my Mercedes for my prime nine o'clock tee time. Come on, what do you think?"

She pulled her phone out of her pocket and accessed her photos. "When I was there yesterday, I took these in one of the maintenance sheds."

He grabbed the cell from her and swiped through the pictures. "If you start wearing a trench coat and shades when you snoop around, I'm either going to stage an intervention or get you a racy red wig so you can disguise yourself as a femme fatale. You could pull it off."

"I'm not responding to that, and I wasn't snooping. I was looking for a bathroom."

"Okay. You say potato, I say potahto. All those stacked bags are different formulations of fertilizer, except for the one that says rye grass. I'm pretty sure that's rye grass."

She kicked his foot again. "Thanks, Einstein."

"Soph, can you try to control her?" He lifted his leg, examining the toe of his boot. "This is the only good pair I have." He rested his foot on the floor and scooted to the sofa's edge. "Back to the business at hand. Some of these formulations, I don't recognize. But this stack of 18-4-18, that's run-of-the-mill grass fertilizer. The three numbers refer to the percentages of nutrients in the mixture. Nitrogen, phosphate, and potash. 12-0-0, that's blood meal."

"What's potash?" Sophia asked. "And is blood meal what it sounds like?"

"Potash is potassium. Standard stuff, and blood meal is exactly what it sounds like. Dried animal blood. It's an organic fertilizer. Country clubs like Whispering Meadows with golf courses are always testing the soil for pH and nutritional needs. The greens are a mix of a variety of grasses that require specific care depending on the season. You know that area of trees I'm clearing out on the front side of the Grove Manor property?"

"Behind the demolition dumpsters?" Olivia said. "I thought that was part of the acreage you sold to that woman last month."

"No. The lot she bought was at the far end. I'm leveling the land and planting grass. Sodding was too expensive, so I hired a landscaping company to seed the entire area. Their plan is to use an 18-24-12 formula to start. They said it was good to promote root development in newly-seeded turf."

"Nutrient wise, that doesn't seem all that different from some of what was in the shed," Olivia said.

"It's not," A.J. confirmed.

"What are you clearing that section for?" Sophia asked.

A.J. loosed a devilish grin while holding a finger to his lips. "It's a surprise and a secret."

Sophia grabbed one of the sofa's decorative pillows and bopped him over the head.

"Hey, what's with you two?" He jokingly cowered like a mouse surrounded by a pair of feisty felines.

Olivia nodded to Sophia. "Permission to fire at will."

She lobbed two more volleys as A.J. deflected the barrage.

"Please, ladies. A bit of decorum befitting your advanced age."

Olivia plucked her phone out of his hand and swiped through the photos. "It sounds like there isn't anything untoward about the products in the shed. What about if the country club used excessive fertilizer? Could runoff from the property leach into the water table and find its way into the lake?"

"Sure. But golf courses have remediation practices in place to prevent that from happening. It would be a public relations nightmare if testing showed Whispering Meadows was poisoning the environment."

"Certainly not ideal when you're vying to become a stop on a national golf tour," Olivia said. "That's a lot of money on the line. Chris mentioned something yesterday about seeing dead fish in the pond on the thirteenth hole at the course. Just like the dead fish we saw at the lake."

"That could be anything, starting with coincidence," A.J. replied. "When I went with your dad to pick up your Expedition last night, we saw a lot of heavy equipment parked in the lot. Backhoes, dump trucks, bulldozers. If I had to guess, I would say they're digging up and moving a lot of dirt."

"Cooper told me about their plans to build a convention center, and it seems Philip Wayne wants to expand his winery and vineyards, preferably with land that is part of Fields Farm. How well do you know Kevin?"

He shook his head. "Not well at all. Chris and I were the same year in high school, but we never hung out together. We ran in different circles. As for Kevin, I just know what I read about him in the papers when he came home after rehabbing from his combat injury."

"Did you know he was engaged to Jenn before he left for his second tour?"

Sophia gasped. "Wait, what? Chris is engaged to his brother's former fiancée. That's messed up."

A.J. nodded. "What she said."

Maria entered the foyer from the hallway, drying her hands with a paper towel. "I thought I heard you two out here. You're both staying for dinner, right?"

"I'll take a rain check," Olivia said.

A.J. stood. "Me, too. I'd love to stay, but I'm grimy from the install. I want to get cleaned up."

"Okay, but don't forget about Saturday. Día de los Muertos. You're both invited to our home." She turned and strode back down the hallway.

"Thanks for setting up the swing. The kids will love it," Sophia said.

"You're very welcome. I know I had a blast when I tested it."

They all said their goodbyes, and Olivia and A.J. left the clinic together. They walked to where she had parked, halfway between Sophia's suite and his office. She unlocked her car, and A.J. opened the driver's door for her.

"I'll call you over the weekend about visiting with Mary on Monday if you still wanna go with me." He held her eyes as if about to speak, but then shifted his gaze to the ground between his feet.

She grinned and goaded him on. "What? Tell me what you were going to say."

He squinted, studied her for a moment, and then let his smile fade. "Truthfully. What's all this about with Daniel?"

"It's nothing, really."

"I see. It doesn't seem like nothing. Flowers? Contacting you now after all this time? Do you want me to beat him up?"

She laughed, playfully shoving his shoulder. "What are you? Ten years old?"

"Ten and a half. Consider it a standing offer."

"I'm more interested in your little secret. What's all this hush-hush about what you're doing out on your property?"

"Okay, Ms. Penn. Trade. You tell me what's really going on with Daniel, and I'll tell you what I'm doing."

"I see. I tell you mine and you tell me yours?"

He nodded. "Exactly."

"You really are ten. Excuse me, ten and a half."

He held up his hands. "Don't say I didn't try to make a deal."

She slid into her seat and fastened her seatbelt.

"Seriously, Liv. Nothing good comes from opening closed doors. Love you. Drive carefully."

"Love you, too, and always."

He shut the door and then waved in her rearview mirror as she pulled away from the curb and headed out of town. As she drove home, she thought of Chris and Kevin, Jenn and Melissa, Jason and Philip. Then there was Daniel. Her head felt muddled, as if lost in its own corn maze. A path here led to two choices there. A turn and a switchback looped her back around to where she had begun. Misdirection and dead ends. Much was uncertain, and there was little guidance offering shortcuts or hints to help solve the puzzle. Where to begin? That much was clear. Tomorrow, she would plumb the depths of the most curious unknown in the equation by finding and speaking with Jason.

CHAPTER 26

Olivia woke up Thursday morning before the first call of her three alarms. She quickly checked for any missed messages, but her phone had slept as soundly as she had throughout the night. She rolled out of bed, gathered fresh clothes, and headed for the shower.

Buddy met her halfway up the steps as she was coming down to start her day. He U-turned and beat her to the bottom.

"You get ready, little guy. We're going for a ride."

He paced to the front door and whipped around, waiting for her to lead the way.

"Not yet. I need breakfast." She swiped his red ball from under a side table and bounced it into the living room, spurring him to scurry after his quarry.

She joined her father in the kitchen, where he was sitting at the table and reading the sports section of the newspaper. "Good morning, Dad."

"Coffee's on."

"Thanks. Smells like you went for a dark roast today. Did you eat breakfast?"

He closed the paper and stood. "No. I'll get something later. I never used to like all these fancy coffees, but these blends you buy are a lot better."

"It's hardly fancy. It's just not instant."

He rinsed his cup out and then dried it with a dish towel. "Nothing wrong with that. That's all I used to drink for years."

"You should eat something in the mornings. At least something small with protein."

He folded the towel and set it on the corner of the counter. "I was going to make scrambled eggs, but some animal must've taken a liking to those chives. The whole patch got ripped up. I'll make soup for lunch. I still have a can of the chunky chicken from the last time it was on sale. I'm leaving now, anyway. I scheduled an appointment at ten for an oil change at Jed's. I'm getting the tires balanced and rotated, too. What about the Expedition? It probably needs an oil change. I'll schedule a time for next week."

She poured cereal into a bowl, grabbed a spoon, and slid both onto the table. "You don't have to. I can do it."

"No, I'll take it. You've got a lot of work to do. Besides, I'm not doing anything except finding more recipes on the internet for things that I'm never going to cook. Although, yesterday, I bookmarked one for a standing rib roast that looked fantastic. I'll send you the link."

She sat and tilted her chair back, opening the refrigerator and removing the almond milk. "I have a meeting in D.C. next week."

"I'll get it done on Saturday then."

"I may not be driving into the office too much anymore."

"Why not?"

"My boss says that the company that owns the paper might make staff cuts soon. She suggested I consider diversifying my repertoire, just in case."

He grabbed his keys from the hook rack and a fleece jacket that was draped over a chair. "What does that mean?"

"I don't know. Broaden my role. Write other columns or features. Maybe go back to being a beat reporter or become an investigative journalist."

He zipped up his jacket and put his keys into one of its pockets. "I don't like the sound of that. You would hate all of those. What about the manuscript you wrote? Have you heard anything back yet from your editor's contact in New York? If that sells, maybe you could become a full-time novelist."

"That doesn't exactly pay the rent. Angela's friend wasn't acting as an official agent for me. He asked me if it was okay if he shared the manuscript with a few of his agent friends who submit to the publishing houses. I said I was fine with that, and I received good feedback. In fact, a couple of people asked me to query them around summer if the manuscript was still available. The guy who was showing my manuscript around—his wife is an editor at one of the major publishers, and she read it and liked it. But I'd still have to go through the proper channels of querying, getting an agent, and submitting the manuscript before it would ever end up on her desk. I'm going to hold on to it right now. Besides, insurance and retirement benefits don't come along with being a novelist."

"Don't give up on your dream. If you want it, I know you'll make it happen." He leaned down and kissed her cheek. "Let's just see how things go. Try not to worry about it. You've been through this kind of thing at work before."

Buddy trotted into the kitchen, carrying his squeaky toy in his mouth.

"I'm going to take him out for his walk," she said.

"Better you than me. The paper says a cold front is coming, and storms may roll through this afternoon. You should go sooner rather than later. I'm off." He opened the kitchen door and exited.

After she had finished her breakfast and cleaned up, she swiped her keys from the counter, grabbed Buddy's leash, and wrestled his toy from him. "Let's try to lose this somewhere." She exited through the kitchen, walked around the garden, and secured Buddy in the rear of her Expedition.

The drive to the lake's access road was an easy, casual

twenty minutes. She turned onto the narrow lane that wound its way to where Jason and Melissa lived. On Tuesday, she had passed Jason's place without taking much notice. A closer view revealed a contemporary, spacious, mobile home equally suitable for someone single or a budding family. The front side had two doors, four windows, and three steps leading to each entrance. A gas grill and a picnic table sat close to the empty patch of matted grass designated as the driveway.

She parked just off the road, got out, and walked past three empty five-gallon plastic buckets on the way to the nearest door. She knocked and waited for half a minute. A drawn shade covered the closest window, preventing any sneak peeks inside. She backed down the steps and strode to the opposite end. The two middle windows were too high for prying eyes, but the fourth one offered a view of a bedroom with a nightstand and a set of dresser drawers.

She shuffled up the mini steps to the second door and knocked. "Hello? Jason?" The worn, wobbly doorknob offered a bit of play. She glanced over her shoulder and then twisted it back and forth, adding a few nudges for good measure. The lock, though, blocked her from criminal breaking and entering.

She returned to her Expedition and onward to the lake. Finding Jason at the park was a long shot, but she was already here, and Buddy needed a walk, anyhow. As she cornered the last turn, Kevin passed by in his SUV, swinging wide to avoid her as he was leaving.

He slowed to a crawl until she had parked, and then he rounded the bend and drove off. The lot was empty except for one other car whose owner who was nowhere around.

She let Buddy out of the back, clipped his leash on his collar, and grabbed his squeaky toy as he sniffed along the ground. They ambled along the trail through the trees leading to the lake. As they arrived at the clearing, Buddy raised his head and tail, alerting her to someone walking on the dock.

Jenn waved, lighting up with a wide, welcoming smile. She stepped onto the shore and briskly paced over to greet them.

"Are you taking this handsome fellow for a walk?" Jenn asked.

"Something like that."

Buddy barked and pawed at Olivia's shins.

"Sit, Buddy." She held him still and shifted his weight onto his hind legs, prompting him to get down. "Stay. Good boy."

Jenn scratched behind his ears. "I have a greyhound. He's a rescue dog and a complete couch potato, but I love him to death. His name is Max. He's Buddha-like calm and so well-mannered."

Buddy sprung up and swiped at Olivia again. She bent forward and unclipped his leash. "I wish I could say the same for this little rascal. Go on, Buddy."

He lolloped off, sniffing and following a scent around the edge of the trail.

"You're not worried that he might run off?"

"No. He'll stay nearby. I brought a secret weapon."

She squeezed his toy, eliciting two short squeaks. Buddy swiveled his head and bounded back to her. He waited for her to throw, but when she lowered the toy to her side, he lost interest and resumed his playful exploration.

"Are you here checking out the bloom?" Olivia asked.

"Yes. It's diminishing for sure. At least in this area, near the dock, and along the water's edge. I haven't walked the entire perimeter of the lake to see if there's growth anywhere else. But this is a good sign. With a quick clearing, I think a temporary environmental factor, rather than leaching contamination, caused it."

"By leaching, do you mean runoff from adjacent land?"

Jenn peeked behind her at Buddy and nodded. "Exactly. Blooms aren't unusual in the early fall when the conditions are right. Warm temperatures, available nutrients in the ecosystem, stagnation of water—they all could be factors."

"You know more about this than anyone. Is it even possible that chemicals used at Whispering Meadows could've caused it?"

Jenn scrunched her eyes. "It's possible, but unlikely. Chris' parents' farm and the golf course both border the park land. There's a stream that runs between the properties and parallel to the lake. Sometimes when we have severe storms, heavy runoff from the stream overflows on the far side and turns that area swampy."

"Does that land abut Whispering Meadows?"

"Yes, but still. Making a case that anything from there caused the bloom would be hard to prove. Besides, it wouldn't even be necessarily illegal. I can't believe they're using anything but what's best for their greens. The farm is certified organic, and we regularly conduct testing to verify our compliance. If the farm violated regulations, it would face major fines."

"If testing showed the farm was the source of the contamination, I assume that would jeopardize the sale," Olivia said.

"I don't know much about the business end. That's Chris' thing. I'm just the resident science nerd. Besides, with the bloom clearing, we'll probably never know what the cause was. What happened to that fieldworker from the VDEQ is far more pressing. To tell you the truth, I was glad when I spotted you on the trail. There's a creepy guy I saw walking around here yesterday. I got a bad vibe from him."

Olivia glanced at Buddy, who was rummaging about in a patch of wildflowers. "This guy you saw. Was he wearing a camouflage jacket?"

"Yeah. You've seen him, too?"

"I think you're talking about Jason Rotterdam. He lives in a mobile home not far up that hill. That's why I'm here. I'm trying to find him."

Jenn shook her head. "Not me. I'm trying to avoid

him. I shouldn't judge, but there was just something about him that made me nervous. Why are you looking for him?"

"I'm following up on a few things. Stuff for the paper. Melissa seems to trust him."

"I met her and her son at the inn yesterday. He's adorable. I take it he's nonverbal. I have a cousin who has epilepsy and is on the autism spectrum. I didn't want to ask, but I recognize the signs."

"I don't know them well either," Olivia said. "She lives down the road from Jason. I think you're right about his speech. I saw Jason use an app on his phone to help him communicate. It seemed to be effective."

"Speaking of communication. I'm going to call a contact at the VDEQ and report the bloom's status. I took pictures to send to him. Protocol would call for a retest, but they might not do so given the police investigation."

Two women approached decked out in high-performance athletic wear. Their swift strides and precise arm pumps suggested they were power walkers embarking on a circuit of the lake. Buddy emerged from the tall grass and followed them for a few footsteps as they passed by.

Olivia watched Buddy, readying to take off after him. "Buddy, stay."

One of the women waved at him. "Hey there, cutie."

He barked and then returned to his adventurous play.

Olivia looked back at Jenn. "What did you think

about the inn? Have you settled on it for your rehearsal dinner?"

She nodded. "Definitely. Bev was super nice to us. She gave me so many options that it'll be hard to decide. I could create a full menu just from the dessert choices alone."

"You won't regret it. The food and ambiance there are wonderful. How's the rest of the planning going?"

"It's overwhelming. The venues are set, but the details are unending." She glanced down at Olivia's hand. "You're not married?"

"No."

"I didn't see a ring, but I didn't want to assume. If you get engaged, call me, and I'll give you a list of everyone I've worked with if you're interested in local vendors."

"Thanks, but I probably won't have a need for anything like that too soon."

"You never know," Jenn said.

A second chance romance? Betrothed to my former flame who I haven't even spoken to in six months? Don't even go there, Liv. She bit back a smile, imagining her and Daniel sitting in a field of tulips under a whirling windmill. He probably would be mansplaining the economic impact the springtime blooms had on Holland's tourist industry. She hoped better for Jenn. "Chris told me you're moving after the wedding."

"Yes. The Netherlands. I still can't believe it. I've only been overseas once, and that was to East Asia for a conference. To think we'll be living there … it's surreal. It's my dream job, and Chris' company has offices in Europe. They've transferred his position there."

"I didn't realize Chris worked for a company. I thought he was involved with the farm on a full-time basis."

"He has been for the past year. But prior to that, he was working remotely here for his employer. The work he did for the farm was on top of that. Back then, it wasn't unusual for him to work eighteen-hour days. When his parents decided to sell, Chris took a leave of absence for a year so he could concentrate on getting the property ready."

Buddy barked, and Olivia glanced over at him exploring in the two-foot-tall wild grass. "What does Chris do?"

Jenn half-turned toward Buddy. "What's that?"

"What is it that Chris does? His company? Who does he work for?"

"No, I mean, what's that?" Jenn pointed at Buddy as he was tugging at something in the grass. She paced toward him, and Olivia followed behind.

Jenn squatted and stroked his back. "What do you have there, fella?" She nudged Buddy aside, stood, and turned, holding a silver metallic case with the VDEQ insignia. She unlatched and opened it, cradling the sides with her arms like an oversized book.

They looked at each other and then at the empty case. Olivia glanced down around the ground where the case had been lying. She bent forward and picked up four blue building blocks.

"Where are all the contents?" Jenn said. "This should be full of testing supplies." She eyed the blocks Olivia held in her palm. "Are those what I think they are? Why would they be here, right by the case?"

"I'm almost positive that these belong to Mikey," Olivia said.

Jenn raised her eyebrows. "Melissa's Mikey? How?"

Olivia nodded, peering toward the far end of the dock. "I'm not sure how, but the lake isn't the only thing that's becoming clearer."

CHAPTER 27

Cole and Bert arrived twenty minutes after Olivia called the police station to report finding the VDEQ case. She and Jenn led the deputies to the patch in the grass where Buddy had sniffed out the evidence. Cole set about photographing and documenting the scene, while Bert bagged the children's blocks and stored the silver case in a white cardboard box. Then he accompanied Olivia and Jenn back to the parking lot, where he questioned each of them separately.

Jenn was up first, and her interview took less than five minutes to complete. When Bert wrapped up his questioning with Olivia, he flipped his spiral notebook shut and slipped his pen into his shirt's chest pocket. "If we need any more information, we'll contact you. You shouldn't be coming out here alone right now. Maybe next time, come with someone for backup."

She jabbed her thumb toward the rear of her Expedition. "I brought my guard dog."

"That little pup? You'd be much safer with a German shepherd."

"Sometimes he thinks he's an FBI K9. He may be little, but he's fierce."

Jenn had been waiting by her car during Olivia's interview, but when the official business had concluded, she strode over to them. "I'm sorry to interrupt. Is it okay if I leave now? I have a presentation for work scheduled soon."

Bert stashed his notebook in his rear pocket. "Yes, ma'am. You're both free to go. And like I said, today or tomorrow, if you'll both come to the station so we can get your prints, we would be much obliged." He smiled slyly at Olivia. "Unless, of course, your fingerprints are already in the system from yesterday."

"No, Bert. They're not. Yesterday was a misunderstanding. I was looking for a bathroom." She turned slightly toward Jenn. "I was involved in a minor incident, but everything got cleared up."

"Gotcha," Bert said. "You two have a good rest of the day." He tipped his hat and strolled back toward the trail leading to the lake.

"I wasn't arrested. It was much ado about nothing. I was at Whispering Meadows and—"

"No need to explain," Jenn said. "I've been on the wrong side of many misunderstandings because of what I do."

"What do you mean?"

"Just that I get attacked by critics who think I care more about the environment than the livelihood of farmers."

"That's harsh," Olivia offered.

"Goes with the territory. There's a balance. I'm trying to develop guidelines for best practices that support both the land and farmers. But many don't see it that way." She checked her watch. "I've got to go. I'll call my contact at the VDEQ and send him the photos later this afternoon. I have to hustle back now to deliver a presentation for a research symposium."

"At the farm?"

"No. It's online. I hate doing this type of event through a screen, but the conference is in California, and I couldn't make it out there right now with the wedding coming up."

"I get that, and I know exactly how you feel."

After they said their goodbyes, Olivia checked in on Buddy. She opened the lift gate, and he raised his head and yawned, rousing from a catnap. He stood slowly, staggered, and shook his body.

"How about some water, little K9? You've gotta be thirsty."

She removed a stainless-steel bowl and a jug of water from a plastic storage cube in the rear compartment. After hoisting him out of the truck and placing him on the ground, she filled the bowl halfway. Buddy lapped

voraciously, and when he had his fill, she dumped out
what remained and shook out the droplets.

She picked him up and settled him back inside. "Stay,
Buddy. We're going home."

He barked as Kevin's SUV rounded the bend and
entered the lot. He parked two car widths from her and
got out, donning his campaign hat while walking toward
her. "I heard you found a case that may have belonged to
the victim."

"Jenn and I did. It was in an area of overgrown grass
right off the lake trail. Police deputies are over there
now." She paused, gauging his flatline reaction. *Time to
poke the beehive.* "We passed each other when I was coming
in. Did you see Jenn when you were here earlier?"

"No. Why would I have?"

She shrugged nonchalantly, mirroring his detached
demeanor. "It just seems you have a common interest—
in the bloom, that is. She was documenting it, and I
assume as a park ranger, you would keep tabs on it, too. I
thought maybe you had arranged to meet—to check on
the bloom."

"No. I didn't arrange anything with her."

Buddy placed his forepaws on the bumper, judging
the distance to the ground. She lifted his front legs and
settled him farther back. "By any chance, have you seen
Jason around here today?" she asked while watching for
any buzzing agitation.

He remained cool and stoic. "Why would you want
to know that?"

She jabbed again. "I need to speak with him."

"Friendly advice. Stay away from Jason."

"Why is that? Melissa trusts him with Mikey. I think that says a great deal about him."

"What is it you're doing here?" he asked.

He's as suspicious of me as I am of him. Interesting. "I came to take my dog for a walk."

"That's not what I meant. You found the victim and now you discover his missing case. You're looking for Jason and questioning Melissa. Chris told me about your meeting with Philip Wayne. You keep showing up in the oddest places."

His bluntness emboldened her to press on. "I wasn't exactly meeting with Mr. Wayne." She glanced down at the ground and kicked some gravel aside. "Since you mentioned Chris. I spoke with him yesterday at the farm. He told me about you and Jenn."

His eyes narrowed, but he didn't blink. "Oh, yeah. What about us?"

"That you two were engaged before your second tour in Afghanistan."

He dipped his chin and diverted his focus off to her side. "That was a long time ago. I was a different person back then. We both were. She's better off with him."

Really? And that's not even a little weird to you? She aimed to keep her tone even, but she couldn't help her own bewilderment. "Your own brother?"

"That's right. She is. I'd still do anything for her. I wouldn't hesitate—"

He thrust his hand into his pants pocket, pulled out a pocketknife, and lunged toward her.

"Whoa, Kevin! Stop! I was just asking about—"

She threw her hands up for defense, and in one violent motion, he swept her behind him. She stumbled as he lowered his stance and snatched a fallen branch off the ground. He jabbed the limb at the grass. "Son of a —" He stabbed again and then reached down.

She backpedaled with her hands high and ready to fight, feeling her pulse pump in her throat. Kevin swiftly spun, displaying an irate snake he had seized below its jaw, as it whipped about, leveraging to strike.

She recoiled and cringed. "Get that away from me!"

He pinned it to the ground, opened his knife with one hand, and severed the head. The mottled brown body continued to wriggle and squirm. He kicked it aside and then poked the thin branch at the triangular head. The fangs clamped down, injecting venom into the limb. He showed her the stick and then tossed it a few feet from him.

Her eyes shifted from the severed head to the twisting body that looked like it was seeking revenge. Sweat dripped down her back, and she flinched at a foraging chipmunk that skittered past her.

"Stay back," Kevin said. "Those fangs can still bite. Copperheads. Nasty buggers." He looked at her while wiping the blood from the knife's blade onto his pants. "They give no warning before they attack. They strike as soon as they feel threatened."

CHAPTER 28

Rattled she had been oblivious to the danger lurking behind her back, Olivia left the parking lot and headed home, still feeling the fight or flight of an adrenaline rush. She hadn't even considered a copperhead may lie in wait, hidden in the grass. A harmless garter snake that had slithered into her backyard tent one night when she was ten instilled a fear of all species of the reptile regardless of if they were venomous. Needing to cool down, she dialed on the air conditioning, and it wasn't until she was halfway home that she realized her left turn signal had been blinking the whole way. Though she was abundantly grateful for Kevin's swift actions, they didn't absolve him from her suspect pool. *He was just doing his job, and I shouldn't have let my guard down like that.* She was even more curious now about his definite dislike of Jason, but that angle would have to be put on hold until after her online Q&A, which was set to start in less than an hour.

She turned onto the lane leading to her house, looking to see if her father's car was in the driveway. He hadn't yet returned, but Jason was there, parked in his pickup in front of their mailbox. She slowly rounded into the driveway and watched in her rearview mirror as he got out of his truck and came toward her. Buddy propped his paws on the rear gate, looked out the window, and growled.

"Quiet, Buddy. Stand down." She unfastened her seat belt, quickly thinking—stay in or get out. In or out. She grabbed her cell, opened the door, and got out.

Jason moseyed up the drive and stopped about ten feet from her. He casually rested his hands in the kangaroo pocket of his camouflage pullover hoodie. "You're looking for me?" he said.

"What would make you think that?"

"Usually, when people are peeping through your windows, it means someone is trying to find you. It's a good thing I lock my doors. You never know who's going to come knocking these days."

She was busted and no manner of hemming and hawing would acquit her of that. *Play it cool.* "So, what, you found me instead? How did you know I live here?"

"The same way you knew where I live."

She had no idea what that meant. "Okay. Here we are, and you want to know why I was looking for you."

He tilted his head and spat off to his side. "I don't care what you want."

This wasn't boding well and appeared to be going nowhere. "Then why are you here?"

"The day that fed guy died—"

"No, he wasn't a fed. His name was Ethan Dunn, and he was a fieldworker from the VDEQ analyzing the algae bloom in the lake."

"He and Kevin argued earlier that morning."

She shifted her weight, taking a subtle step back. "Okay, and?"

"Ranger Rick isn't stable."

"I'm sorry, but you've lost me."

"That morning, Melissa and Mikey were down by the dock talking to that guy, and Kevin got all bent out of shape because of it."

"And you know this how?"

"I had plans to fix a faucet in Melissa's kitchen, but when I got there, she wasn't home. I knew that she and Mikey go for walks sometimes in the mornings, so I went down to the lake to meet them."

"What are you getting at?" she asked.

He took a step closer. "I'm saying Kevin almost fought with Dunn, and I had to separate them."

"I'm sure the police know this."

He shook his head. "I'm sure they don't."

"Why is that?"

"Melissa wouldn't want to bring suspicion on Kevin, which would be easy to do, given his past."

Her flight reflex grumbled. She wanted to end this, preferably with a locked door between them." She drew her shoulders back and brushed by him to the rear of her truck. As soon as she opened the liftgate, Buddy climbed onto the bumper.

"Look, Jason, this has been a great chat, but I think you should be on your way. I'm not sure why you're telling me this. Come on, Buddy. I've got you." He barked as she lifted him, and she spun, sensing Jason step closer.

"I'm telling you this because Kevin and Melissa are together."

Buddy licked her face, and she angled her chin away and then set him on the ground. He paced a few feet toward the house, but then returned to her side, slowly sweeping his tail. She bent down and gently nudged him aside. "Go on. Get going." She stood tall as he playfully pranced about in the front yard.

"You mean Kevin and Melissa are a couple?"

He nodded. "That's right."

"Okay. I still don't know why you're telling me this."

"Because the ranger is a loose cannon. I'm worried about Melissa and Mikey whenever he's around. Sometimes, the answer to the puzzle isn't all that complicated. Somebody working inside the police station is ignoring the elephant in the room."

"Are you suggesting that Kevin had something to do with Dunn's death?"

"I know he does."

She shook her head without a second thought. He was peddling snake oil, and she wasn't about to bite.

"Why are you telling me? Didn't you report this to the police when they questioned you?"

He paused, softening his stance. "Melissa asked me not to. Do you think they'd take my word over his, anyway? They'll notice, though, when a reporter asks questions. There's a cover-up happening and—" He stopped, focusing over her shoulder.

She closed the rear door and turned, following his eyes.

Sam had crossed over from her yard and was walking toward them carrying a pitchfork. "Hey, Liv. I was loosening some soil around my flower beds. Everything okay over here?"

"Hi, Sam. Yeah, everything's fine. We're just talking."

Jason turned and walked back to his truck.

Olivia trailed behind him, keeping her distance. "What happened between you and Crescent Valley Organics?"

He opened his door and stared at her as she stood at the bottom of the driveway. "Do you know Kevin works security on weekends at Whispering Meadows?" he asked. "The answer to everything is money. It's all about the money." He got into his truck, shut the door, and drove off.

Sam stepped to Olivia's side. "Was that the guy from the lake that you told me about?"

"Yes. Jason Rotterdam. I went to find him this morning, but he found me instead. Thanks for coming over. Sorry to take you away from your yard work."

"No, not at all. I was throwing out the trash, and I saw you two over here. I didn't like the looks of him. I thought you could use backup." She held up the pitchfork. "And I brought a friend."

Olivia smiled at Sam's honed situational awareness. "I appreciate that. I'm glad my dad wasn't here to witness this."

"What did he want? What was he talking about when he said the answer to everything was money?"

Olivia shrugged her shoulders. "Honestly, I'm not sure. But if the answer is money, there's got to be a trail."

CHAPTER 29

With her online Q&A scheduled to start soon, Olivia hustled to get inside, wanting to grab a snack and soda to help her endure the spotlight of the coming hour. Buddy was sitting at the top of the porch and staring at her skeleton decor, which was upside down at the bottom of the steps. She picked up the figurine, walked up onto the porch, and placed it on the small bistro table. Buddy popped up and barked as she pulled two chairs out of his climbing range.

"Let's see you get at it now."

She opened the front door, locked it, and shooed him into the living room. After a quick trip through the kitchen to gather her provisions, she went out the back and hurried to her office.

Once inside, she set her drink and a Granny Smith apple on her desk and then booted up her laptop. Her phone chimed with a text: "Five-minute warning."

She shot off a reply: "I'm with you. Give me a few seconds."

Just as she hit send, her cell rang. She slipped in her wireless earbuds that she always used to chat with Angela during the online Q&A's.

"Hey, Angela. I'm almost ready."

"I wanted to run something by you."

Olivia opened her soda, misting her hand with fizz. "This can't be good, but go ahead."

"Two words. Video stream."

"Of what?"

"These weekly, I mean biweekly, chats."

"Oh, Angela. No. Absolutely not."

"Wait, Olivia. Hear me out."

"Don't waste your breath. The answer is no. You know I don't like these chats, period. A video stream? You can't be serious."

"What's the difference? You'd be doing the same thing. Video is king. Imagine—Ms. Penn in her natural habitat. Streaming real time reactions. Uncensored. Uncut."

"That sounds like I'd either be a circus act or a carnival sideshow. The line's blurry, but they're equally disturbing and reviling."

"Don't be such a negative Nelly. Just run a comb through your hair. And would it kill you to put on some mascara?"

"No, Angela. Final answer."

"Let's keep the door open. Have you given any thought to what we talked about yesterday?"

She leaned back, rocking in her chair. "Yes, but I don't have an answer for you yet. I get what you're saying. I know you're looking out for me, and I'm grateful. I'm considering your advice. New York is off the radar, though. I don't want to be that far away from my dad now. I need more time to think about it." She paused for a moment as her mind drifted to what Jason had said just a few minutes ago about elephants in the room. "Here's a random question for you. What do you know about organic farming?"

"That's a bizarre question. I can check with the food section editors to see if they're interested, but they're running mostly recipes these days rather than features. When I suggested diversifying, I didn't mean switching to write a recipe or food column. They already have staff for that."

"No. That's not what I meant."

"Oh. Wait, are you raising chickens now? I hear that's all the rage among city folk who turn country. You're not wearing coveralls, are you? Come to think of it, that might be cute on camera."

She logged onto the chat. "Not yet on either count. Forget I asked."

"Okay. I see you now on the feed. It'll just be another minute."

Olivia slid a tablet toward her from the corner of the desk, propped it up on its kickstand, and opened a browser. She cross-referenced Crescent Valley Organics and Jason Rotterdam. The results returned many of the same articles she had perused before. Then the first question for the online Q&A popped up on the laptop screen.

Candy Apple Red: Sis just got engaged, and I'm pregnant. We both want to announce at Thanksgiving to our parents, but she feels I'm trying to upstage her. I think it's time to get over the sibling rivalry. Thoughts?

Ms. Penn: You each deserve your moment. When in doubt, go first. She's announcing an event to come. You're announcing something that already is. Go first, the week or a few days before. You won't be dividing your parents' joy. You'll be doubling it. Congrats to you both.

As she waited for the next question in the feed, she searched for anything related to Chris Fields and Virginia. Fifteen million results appeared in half a second. She refined the query, drilling down the location to Apple Station. The results page populated with snippets mostly from agricultural news sites along with a few articles from the *Apple Station Times*. She scanned for the most recent dates and then glanced over at her laptop screen.

Shape Shifter Vamp: Is lying by omission to protect someone's feelings ever okay?

Ms. Penn: Lying by omission isn't the same as a white lie. White lies are over trivial matters to spare someone's feelings. Example: Your child asks after his first violin lesson, "How did I sound?" You answer, "Perfect! Like music from heaven." Lying by omission is intentionally hiding information to deceive. Quoting poet Adrienne Rich, "Lying is done with words and also with silence."

Pop Goes the Weasel: My husband bought me a gym membership for my birthday, which I didn't want. I don't even work out. I'm furious. Should I say something?

Olivia glanced back at her tablet and switched the results to pull up images associated with her search. Most were from Chris Fields namesakes. She recognized one, though, from the farm, with him standing beside a pumpkin-chucking cannon wearing a red sweatshirt. She enlarged the photo for a better view of a prominent white "W" and a mascot logo on the front. She drew her fingers apart, increasing the magnification. "I don't believe it."

"I know, poor woman," Angela said.

"That's a badger."

"That's not the first name I'd call the husband, but whatever, you're the pro."

"That's a University of Wisconsin badger," Olivia said. "That's a weird coincidence. I wonder …"

"What are you talking about?" Angela asked.

She looked back at the question waiting for her on the laptop's screen.

Ms. Penn: Happy birthday to you! Treat yourself. Sometimes we must give to ourselves what others can't or won't give to us. Should you say something? Definitely. Thank him for the membership and tell him you're working with a highly skilled and extremely buff personal trainer whose only concern is your satisfaction. His name is Rhett, and he's offered to be your golf instructor as well —because he's a pro with a smooth and powerful swing.

She searched for a connection between Chris and Crescent Valley Organics. Four hundred thousand results turned up in under three-quarters of a second. A quick scroll down the first page revealed useless bits about any random Chris associated with an organic farm in a valley. She narrowed her search to Wisconsin and clicked on the top result. The opening paragraph began: "Chris Fields, Research Director for Emerging Technology, reports promising findings from...."

"He works for them," she said.

"What did you say, Olivia? Who?"

"Chris Fields works for Crescent Valley Organics."

"Olivia, what are you talking about? Are you having a stroke?"

"I'm so sorry, Angela, but I have to go."

"No-no-no, Olivia. Don't you go anywhere. Don't you dare."

"Angela, my screen froze. I have to reboot the router. This could take a while. Cover for me."

"Olivia! I swear if you leave, I'll make it my life's mission to ensure this becomes a video stream."

"I'll fight you on that. Thanks, Angela. I'll explain later."

She shut her laptop, pocketed her phone, and headed for her Expedition.

CHAPTER 30

As Olivia backed out of the driveway, she debated whether to call Preston's cell or stick to official channels and contact him through the police station's nonemergency line. This was business, not personal. Then again, they had no personal business. She had called him only once about something not related to police work, and that had been to give him the measurements of the front porch's side railing. Still, she had starred his phone number as one of only a handful of favorites under her contacts. She came to a stop sign and tapped his teddy bear avatar. When he answered, she spoke hands free.

"Hi, Preston. This is Olivia. Where are you?"

"Excuse me?" he asked. "Why would you want to know that, and why would I tell you? And I know it's you. You don't need to introduce yourself."

"Can we meet someplace?" she said. "I want to run something by you."

He paused, as if distracted. "I'm on my way out. I can't talk or meet with you right now."

She turned onto the two-lane road leading into town. "Did you know Chris works for Crescent Valley Organics? That's the company that's about to buy his parents' farm."

"The real question, Olivia, is why do you know that? Believe it or not, we are the police. This is kind of our thing. Not yours."

"Why didn't you say something?"

"To whom? You? Do I need to even answer that? What are you doing?" His voice lowered. "Jayden, I'm leaving now. Call me if you get a hold of them."

She veered slightly around a bicyclist straddling the shoulder of the road. "I just wanted to see if you knew about Chris."

"Sorry. I missed that. What did you say?" he asked.

"Nothing. I ... ah ..."

"Olivia, I know you're still digging into all of this, and I don't know if this is you being a journalist and wanting to break a headline grabbing story—"

"No, not at all."

"Then tell me why. Because I don't understand why you would even put yourself in any danger. Your father wouldn't want that. I don't want that. This investigation doesn't involve you."

"I'm not doing anything illegal, and I'm not interfering with your business. Sometimes, people will speak more openly with a reporter who listens to their side of the story than they will with the police. I'm only trying to help. What I learn I pass on to you." *Eventually.* It was a tenuous, half-hearted rebuttal, but she hoped it was enough to placate him. Before he could counter, she changed the subject. "Chris told me about what you did for Kevin. He said you helped him enroll in the park ranger program."

His truck door slammed shut and, within seconds, country music blared. He swore and turned the volume down. "Sorry about that. Kevin's a great guy, but he had a difficult time adjusting when he returned home after his rehab at Walter Reed."

"But how are you connected to him?"

He paused, allowing silence to hold the space between them, and then continued. "I know I can trust you not to spread old gossip. One night, Kevin got into a bar fight in Luray and busted up some guy's face. A buddy of mine in the Luray Police Department was in Kevin's Ranger company during his second tour. My friend persuaded the victim not to press charges, since the brawl involved a woman who wasn't the guy's wife. Later that week, my friend contacted me and asked if I had any local connections that could use someone with Kevin's skill set. I made some inquiries and called a few people. That's all. Kevin did all the hard work, physically and mentally healing."

"What exactly is his skill set?"

"Kevin wanted to be career military. Rangers are elite and mission oriented, trained to defend the country and fight with their comrades. Surrender isn't a Ranger word. Kevin drifted when he came back. He didn't have the same sense of purpose that he had before his injury. But he's a different person now. He likes his job, and he does it well. He's dependable, and I trust him to have my back in a jam."

"You don't think he's capable of violence, do you?" she said.

"Why would you ask that?"

"I've seen his temper, and he's pretty handy with a knife." She related his swift and violent elimination of the snake at the lake.

"It sounds like he saved you from a trip to the ER. Copperhead bites aren't fatal, but they're not pretty."

She arrived in town and parked in a spot by the inn. "Do you know he's dating Melissa?"

"I don't keep up on your social column."

"My what?"

"I'm just kidding. Kevin disclosed his relationship with Melissa on Monday when we were collecting evidence at the lake. Was there anything else you needed?"

She watched as he pulled away from the curb in front of the police station, unsure of whether to tell him about her weird meeting with Jason. She was still on the fence herself, not knowing if that conversation was something or nothing. "No, that was it."

"I've got to go. I'll call Kevin later to check in to see how he's doing. And Olivia, stay out of the investigation."

"Like I said, Preston, I'm not interfering or digging for a headline."

"I'll take your word for it then. And for the record, I may have read a few of your columns."

She smiled, eyeing his truck as he turned onto Blossom Avenue. "Thank you. Be sure to like and subscribe to my feed so you never miss a post."

He laughed over the three-quarter time of a slow country waltz. "Bye, Olivia."

The line went silent, and she peeked at the screen until his teddy bear avatar vanished. *I wasn't lying to him. I'm not interfering, but it's all there in front of me. Somebody's hiding in plain sight. This went from smelling fishy to death tomb reeking in a hot second. If I could just connect the dots. I'm so close, I can feel it.*

The town square was undergoing its temporary transition from a charming community gathering spot to a spooky, haunted Halloween trail for tomorrow's costume parade. Hay bales lined the route, and cheerful crews of volunteers were decorating each of the trick-or-treating stops along the way. Near to her, four scarecrows eerily loomed over a pumpkin patch. Their raggedy threads had seen better days, and they were tethered in place, unable to run away. Their arms were spread wide as if ready to shout, "Happy Halloween!" But they had no mouths. *Poor fellas. They have arms but no legs.*

She opened her photos to look at the picture she had taken of Mikey's drawing. She was like the scarecrow, missing legs. She enlarged the photo, scrolled, and re-centered. She could only study a small section at a time, and each part considered in isolation didn't make sense. She thought of the big picture, of the elephant in the room, of the answer to everything being money.

"I'm not seeing the forest for the trees. I need to see this entire picture again, all at once." She jumped out of her car, locked up, and hurried to the newspaper's office.

CHAPTER 31

Olivia barreled into the office, beelining for the copier stationed outside of Ellen's closed door. Cooper glanced up from his desk as he licked and sealed an envelope. He piled it on top of a neatly aligned, sizable stack and then greeted her with a wave.

"Hey, Olivia. Envelope glue is gross. I don't know why we can't buy self-stick ones. They're not that expensive. My mom wants to speak with you."

She stopped dead in her tracks, pointing to Ellen's office.

"No, she's not in now," he said. "She went to the inn for a final planning meeting for the fundraiser. That's what she says, anyway. They're just having lunch while I stuff envelopes for them and consume glue. Can't you get high on glue?"

"Different type of glue. You'll be fine. I was never here. You didn't see me."

He licked another envelope. "You were never here now, standing in front of me?"

She nodded. "Right. Got it?"

He picked up his completed stack and dropped them in an outgoing mail bin on his desk. "Oh, I get it. Secret stuff. My lips are sealed tighter than these envelopes."

She stepped to the copier, pulled out her cell, and studied the options on the control panel. "Is this thing hooked up to the Wi-Fi? Can I print from my phone?"

"Yeah, just connect to the network." He joined her by the all-in-one office machine, checked the paper tray, and then loaded a ream.

She typed in the office password, connected, and printed Mikey's drawing.

Cooper crumpled the copy paper's wrap and then shot a basket at the bin. "That's an odd drawing. What's that for?"

"This stays between us. Understand?"

He winked, lighting up with a furtive smile. "Absolutely, chief."

She held the paper between them. "This is a picture that Mikey Barns, Melissa's son, drew the day I found Ethan Dunn in the lake. Do you know Melissa?"

"A little. She works part-time at the library, mostly on Saturdays. She always saves me the latest cozies when they come in."

She gave him a slight grin.

"As in mysteries," he added.

"No, I get it. I read them, too." She angled the paper toward him. "What do you see here?"

He narrowed his eyes, pointing to each object as he named them. "People, trees, house, lake."

"And how many people do you see?"

"One, two, three, four." He tapped the horizontal stick figure at the end of the dock. "Is that the dead dude? I mean the victim. Am I supposed to count him, too?"

"Yes, that's Dunn, and no, don't count him. What about these?"

"Easy peasy. Two animals and two cars."

"That's easy? How do you know those are cars?"

He drew his brows together, scrutinizing the drawing again. "Oh, am I wrong? What do you think they are?"

"No, you're actually right, according to the police."

"Four people, three trees, two cars, a house, and a partridge in a pear tree." He smiled as he straightened his paisley print tie. "Sorry, that was insensitive. What are you thinking?"

She studied the drawing, tracing her finger from the dock to where she was supposedly walking with A.J. and Buddy. "When the police first showed me this, the working theory was that Mikey saw me twice on Monday. First when I was with A.J. and then when I found Dunn. If we accept the premise that this is what he observed, then this picture represents everything. Two moments of time in the same drawing."

Cooper's face blanked. "I'm not following."

SILENCE SAYS THE MOST

She tapped the square on the dock. "There was no square. There was no box."

He leaned closer to the page. "What's the square?"

"That's it, Cooper. There was no box." She folded the paper, stuffed it into her pocket, and stepped toward the entrance. "Thanks, Cooper."

"Are you going to tell me what all that means?"

She turned, walking backward toward the door. "I've got to check something out to know for sure. And remember, you never saw me."

He nodded. "I'll tell my mom that you absolutely were not in while she was away, supposedly planning the fundraiser."

She left the office, hopped into her Expedition, and peered across the town square. Sophia was standing on the sidewalk in front of her clinic, waving goodbye to a mother and her child. When Sophia ducked back inside, Olivia dialed her cell.

"Hey, Liv. What's up?"

"You've worked with Mikey before, so you know him pretty well, right?"

"Since you already know I have, I can say yes. But I can't discuss any specifics about him. Are you working now?"

"Not exactly. I'm across the town square."

"Where? I'm looking out the window. I don't see you."

"I'm sitting in my car outside the newspaper's office."

"Oh, there you are. Why are you calling me from your car when I can literally see you?"

"How well does Mikey recognize people?"

"What do you mean? And why are you even asking? Are you going to come over?"

"If Mikey saw a picture of someone that he's familiar with, would he know who they are?"

"I don't know. I'm not speaking specifically about Mikey here, but I can say it's common for children on the autism spectrum to have facial agnosia. That's when you can't recognize faces. Even familiar faces they see every day. Mother, father, brother, sister. They may not even recognize themselves in a mirror. But Mikey is much smarter than many give him credit for. He's very observant. He understands more than he can express. Where are you going with all of this?"

She started the engine and fastened her seatbelt. "I think Mikey saw who killed Dunn, and he took evidence from the scene."

"Whoa, back up. Stay where you are. I'm coming over. Or you come here."

"I'm going to Melissa's house to speak with her now."

Sophia stepped out of the clinic and onto the sidewalk. "She's not there."

"How do you know?"

"Because she's with my mom at the fundraiser meeting at the inn. Don't go anywhere yet. Come over to the clinic."

"Is Mikey with her?"

"No. Melissa stopped by before the meeting to talk with me about the benefits of therapy. I asked her where he was, and she said that she didn't want to bring him to the inn because of how it threw him off his routine last time."

"Do you have any idea who's watching him now at the house?"

"She said Kevin was."

Olivia pulled away from the curb. "Thanks, Soph."

"Wait, Liv. Where are you going?"

"Gotta go. I'll call you back later." She lowered her window and waved at Sophia as she headed out of town.

CHAPTER 32

Pushing right to the speed limit, Olivia hightailed her way to Melissa's house to confirm her suspicions. She glanced at her cell on the passenger seat and had an inkling to call Preston. *It would take longer to explain to him than to find out if I'm right. I'm just a few minutes away. If I'm wrong, so be it. No harm, no foul, and I'll back off.*

The two-lane road connecting the town to the park shot straight as an arrow, except for a section in the middle that twisted in a tricky, tight S-curve. The straightaways on either side lulled those unprepared for the sudden double misdirection. Unsuspecting drivers and those that didn't heed the warning signs often found themselves crashed or plunged into a ditch. After rounding the curve's last bend at a snail's pace, she ramped back up to speed along the straightaway leading to the lake.

There was no traffic ahead to hinder her progress,

and only two other cars were in sight, both pulled over on the opposite shoulder. The lead car was in distress with its drivers-side rear elevated by a jack. As she raced by, her focus briefly locked on the rescue vehicle parked right behind it.

Her eyes darted to her rearview mirror, and with no one bearing down, she slammed on the brakes and stopped in the middle of the road. She lowered her window and looked back. Kevin was kneeling on the ground, twisting a tire iron to remove lug nuts from a flat.

She U-turned, using the full shoulder width of the oncoming lane, and then pulled up close to his bumper. After a peek back for oncoming vehicles, she opened the door, slid down from her seat, and hastened toward him. "What are you doing here?" she asked.

"That was an illegal U-turn you just made," Kevin said matter-of-factly as he tugged the tire iron away from the rim. "If you've come to assist, I think I have this under control."

She glanced behind at his SUV. "Where's Mikey?"

He set the tire iron on the ground and stood, looking toward a young woman and a child standing on a slope at a safe distance from the road. "Excuse me, ma'am. I'll be right back. You two stay up there." He wiped his hands on his uniform pants and then grabbed Olivia's elbow and led her onto the grass farther away from the shoulder. "Why are you asking about Mikey?"

"It's just that I heard you were supposed to be watching him while Melissa was at the inn."

"Not that it's any of your business, but I was. Mikey was napping when my brother stopped by."

"Why did he come? Did he know you were there?"

"What's this about?" he demanded.

A tractor trailer zoomed by, scattering the newly fallen leaves lying on the road. Kevin glared at the rig's rear. "Idiot. Driving that fast on this stretch, right ahead of that curve." He turned back toward her. "No. Chris didn't come to see me. He came for Melissa. He brought her a pumpkin pie he said was from my mother. It was something about my mother seeing her and Mikey at the maze yesterday. I don't know the full story, and I really don't care. Look, I've got to fix this flat tire and get them off the shoulder before we have an accident here. I was on my way to Whispering Meadows when I saw they needed help, so I stopped. But I need to hurry out there. I received a call about a coyote roaming the golf course, and it may need to be darted. Animal control is en route, but I'm a better shot than anyone they'd be sending." He checked his watch. "Melissa should be home soon. Mikey's fine. My brother is watching him."

She nodded as the last puzzle piece clicked for her. "Yes, of course. I'm sorry to keep you."

He watched as a sedan slowly passed by, veering over the center double yellow line to grant the three parked vehicles a wide berth. "Melissa told me you took Mikey through the corn maze yesterday at the farm. Thank you for helping her out. She has a lot on her plate right now. She's an excellent mother."

"Yes, she is. I'm glad I could help."

He looked toward the jacked car. "Well, I should ..."

"Yes. Thanks for your time," she said. "Be safe." She hurried back to her Expedition and jumped in. *That's it. Chris, the move, the sale ... yes, this all makes sense. Mikey's blocks. Thank you, Mikey, for leaving those blocks behind.* She reversed a few feet, checked both ways for oncoming traffic, and U-turned, speeding straight away for Melissa's.

CHAPTER 33

Olivia passed Jason's mobile home without a second thought. His pickup was missing and drawn white slat shades covered all four front windows. Whether he was there or watching from elsewhere no longer concerned her. She rounded the bend to Melissa's cottage, focusing instead on the black luxury sedan parked close to the house at the top of the dirt driveway. She pulled up and stopped as near to the rear bumper as she dared, partially pinning the vehicle to hinder any attempt at a hasty departure. After snatching her cell, she slipped down from her seat and eased her door shut.

She tiptoed up the steps, peered inside through the open door, and knocked on the screen's metal frame. "Hello? Chris, Mikey?" She inched the screen open, provoking an eerie squeak from the rusty hinge. "Anyone here?"

She stepped inside, letting the screen bang shut

behind her. Her eyes shifted, homing in on the living room floor. Someone had dumped the contents of the coffee table storage bin, leaving building blocks, metal cars, and crayons strewn across the rug. She glided over to the items, knelt on both knees, and scanned a three-sixty view, searching for the vials she had seen on Tuesday.

She leaned down to check under the couch, spotting more blocks, a small squishy sensory ball, and something else she couldn't quite make out toward the back. As she drew her cheek closer to the narrow gap for a better view, a floorboard in the hallway creaked. She sprung up tall on her knees and chanced a peek over the sofa. Then a second, shorter crack sounded from farther back. She scrambled to her feet and stood statue-still, listening for any further noises.

She quietly padded to the hallway. Two doors aligned on each side. She paced forward and inched open the first door on the left, revealing a tidy linen closet teeming with toiletries and towels. She crossed to the opposite wall, keeping to the wood flooring's less worn edges. The door was open, and she readily found and flipped on a switch, illuminating a full bathroom swathed in muted green. A bin of bath toys rested on the floor by the tub, and a diffuser on the top shelf of a corner cabinet dispersed the essence of lavender. She stepped to the next room on the right. Melissa's bedroom, she surmised by the furnishings: a queen bed, two dressers, and a full-length standing mirror.

The last door on the left offered a quarter view. She crept forward, shifting her weight discreetly from heel to toe. A white mini tent was pitched beside a racing car bed, surrounded by soothing powder blue walls. The late afternoon sun filtered through a window, infusing Mikey's room with a tranquil, warm glow. She swallowed hard, took a deep breath, and pushed the door wider to expand the view. She peeked inside without stepping farther. Plastic storage bins lined the opposite wall, and a padded mat with a pillow and headphones lay on the floor by the foot of his bed.

She backpedaled, staring down the hallway, and listened. No noise, no movement, no signs of life. She pivoted and glided silently toward the living room, where she scanned the front yard through the window. All appeared much the same as it had on Tuesday, though Mikey's bike now was lying on its side by the luxury sedan.

She stepped outside and prowled through the yard to the rear of the cottage. A stout breeze blew through, scattering speckled, dead leaves from the branches of the surrounding, towering oak trees. The lake shone through the thinned-out forest, and the trail from the house was visible from top to bottom. She swept the scene as far as she could see. Her eyes locked on a flash of red darting toward the path's lakeside end.

She bolted and barreled down the hill after Mikey, rustling and strewing leaves as she picked up speed. "Mikey, wait! Stop!"

CHAPTER 34

By the time Olivia had cleared the trees, Mikey was running along the lake trail, heading toward the dock. She shortcut through the wildflowers and quickly caught up. She grasped his shoulders to slow him, but he squirmed and wiggled, trying to slip his arms from his jacket's sleeves.

"Mikey, hold on." She dropped to a knee and wrangled him in close. "Mikey, it's okay. Remember me?"

He loosed a high-pitched shriek and rocked from side to side. She fished her phone from her pocket and swiped open the video app she had used with him in the corn maze. The same cartoon still topped the recently played list. She held the cell close to his eyes and hit play.

"Look, Mikey." A bouncy jingle sounded, and dancing bears animated the screen.

He stilled, stared, and settled.

"That's it. See, everything's okay."

He stretched for the phone, patting her hand.

"Hold on. Let me check your pockets." She reached into one, finding four blue building blocks. Then she rummaged through the other and discovered the three vials she had come seeking.

Mikey glanced over her shoulder, grunted, and coiled his arm around her neck. She swiveled as Chris was fast approaching, mirroring her shortcut through the wildflowers.

He smiled and waved while walking toward them. "Olivia, thank goodness he's with you."

She unwrapped Mikey's arm, stood, and grabbed his hand. Drawing him close to her side, she paced backward a few feet.

"It's my fault. He was napping, and I totally forgot what Kevin said about setting the door alarms. I stepped outside to take a business call, and he must've slipped out when I had my back turned. I've been looking for him everywhere."

She held up her hand. "That's far enough, Chris."

He kept advancing. "What's that, Olivia?"

"Why did you come to see Melissa?"

He laughed nervously as his pace slowed. "I'm just glad you showed up. You must think I'm completely irresponsible. I guess I have a lot to learn before becoming a parent. I'll take him back home."

"Stay there, Chris. Don't come any closer."

His thin smile flatlined as he stalked forward. "What's

going on? Let me explain. I think there's a misunderstanding here."

She quickened her backpedal, holding tight to Mikey's hand. As they neared the dock, she woke her phone with her thumb and tapped open her contacts.

"Who are you calling? I already contacted Melissa. She knows."

"I doubt that. How about I call Jenn?"

His jaw hardened. "Why would you do that?"

"To let her know you couldn't find what she sent you to look for."

He glanced behind him and then scanned the lake's near-side perimeter. "I'm not sure I'm following you. She's at home, packing for a last-minute flight to the Netherlands. The university invited her to be a stand-in for a no-show at an international symposium on the future of organic farming."

"Is that so? I just saw her this morning, and she didn't mention anything about that."

He cleared his throat and checked all around again. "It's getting a little chilly out here. I think we should get Mikey home before Melissa returns."

She continued pacing backward and peeked at her screen, locking on Preston's avatar.

His eyes narrowed as his brow furrowed, exposing his concern. "Who are you calling?"

She hit connect, spun, and yanked Mikey forward as she broke out into a run.

Chris launched after her and caught up within a few strides. He clutched her arm and tugged back hard. The violent about-face snapped her hold on Mikey's hand. Chris seized her elbow, but she slipped free. Mikey remained close by, waving his hands while screaming. She flashed her cell past his eyes. Then she stepped forward, shifted her weight, and hurled her phone toward the trail leading to his house with all the strength that she had. Mikey's sight followed the flight, and then he darted after it.

Chris watched Mikey for a moment, then turned and faced her. She scurried back, luring him away from chasing after Mikey. *Come after me.* He stepped toward her. *That's right, keep coming.*

"Mikey can't tell the police what he saw, but I'll tell them exactly why you risked coming to Melissa's house to protect your fiancée.

He lunged at her, and she ducked and dashed. He caught her from behind and shoved her forward. She lost her footing and fell to the ground, rolling several times before coming to a stop at the foot of the dock.

CHAPTER 35

After scrambling to her feet at the edge of the dock, Olivia looked toward where she had fired her phone. Her scraped palms stung, and her shoulder twinged from her rough, precipitous tumble. Mikey was standing still, facing uphill and staring at something he held close to his face. She was still startled from the fall and had no easy avenue for escape. Her only goal in the moment was to separate Mikey from Chris. And although she didn't want Mikey to be alone, he was safer now than he would be at her side. *Please go home, Mikey. Please, just start walking away.*

Chris looked at Mikey and then scanned all around. He closed the space between them with his hands held high, vying to control and calm the scene. "Easy, now. Let's just talk for a second. I don't know what you think is going on here. You have it all wrong."

She glanced back at Mikey, who was near to where the path to his house led into the trees. *That's it. Good, Mikey. Keep walking. Go home.* "You work for Crescent Valley Organics."

"I know how that looks, but there's really nothing to it. This sale is a good deal for my parents and for the company. Everyone wins."

"Especially you and Jenn. You'll get your share of the proceeds, plus what? Are you receiving some sort of bonus from Crescent Valley for brokering the sale? Is that the arrangement you have?"

Chris looked toward the trail leading to the park's front side. "I'm not sure what you're getting at."

She estimated ten minutes had passed since she connected her call. Did it go through? Would Preston call back or surmise something was wrong? Mikey had walked into the forest leading to his home. *It should take him just a few minutes for him to get back if he went straight there.* Would Melissa return home to find Mikey alone or missing with two strange cars in her driveway? Would she contact Kevin? Would she call the police?

Olivia looked up and down the trail, and then peeked over her shoulder at the runway she knew well from her cannonballing days. She couldn't outrun Chris, but she was confident she could outswim him.

"Your parents don't know, do they? How is it that the farm's production and value increased so much in such a short time since you and Jenn took over managing the land?"

His nostrils flared. "What are you getting at? What do you think you can prove?"

She clenched her fists, readying to turn for takeoff. "Jenn sent you to search for those sampling vials from the testing kit. The ones that Mikey had removed from the case. What happened, Chris? She must've gotten spooked on Monday after she killed Dunn. She needed to leave the scene quickly, but it would've been too risky for her to be seen carrying that case by anyone who might be on the park's front side. So, she stashed it and thought she would return to retrieve it. She had to because she left her fingerprints at the crime scene of a murder. But the vials were missing when we found the case, and she deduced correctly that Mikey had taken them because I told her the blocks we found belonged to him."

Chris shook his head. "No. None of that's true. You're wrong. Jenn doesn't have anything to do with this."

Olivia looked again for anyone who could hear her scream and then continued. "You and Jenn came searching for the case on Tuesday, but the police were already here. She returned yesterday and today, but not to take pictures of the algae bloom. She desperately needed to find the case, but she couldn't because Mikey had moved it—"

"No. Stop. You don't know what you're talking about." His eyes widened as his cheeks flushed scarlet red.

"I bet Jenn's not planning on stopping by the police

station before she leaves. Her fingerprints must already be in the system. I'm sure the police will find three matching sets of prints on those vials and on the case. Dunn's, Mikey's, and hers."

He held up his hands again, nodding as his chest heaved. "Let's work something out. I have money." His breathing intensified, increasing in depth with each step. "No one has to know. Help me get those vials, and you can name your price. Everyone has a price, including you. We can keep this to ourselves. Whatever you want, it's yours."

She paced backward onto the dock.

He closed in and continued, "Please, Jenn didn't mean to do it. I'm begging you. She panicked. It's a waste of her talent for her to be locked up for the rest of her life because of a mistake. Please, let's just work something out."

"She murdered Dunn."

"It was an accident. I swear to you."

She shuffled back two measured steps, landing on a frail board that creaked under her feet. "Jenn must've been afraid of what those samples would show. Why is that?"

He lunged toward her, and she spun and sprinted down the dock. In seconds, she would have to leap as she had when she was a child and swim faster than she ever had before in her life. She slowed slightly as she neared the edge, judging her trajectory. She took a deep breath, prepared to jump, and peeked behind her one last time. Her head snapped forward as Chris launched her off her feet, and together, they plunged into the lake.

CHAPTER 36

Chris submerged Olivia in the silence of the cold, dark water. She flailed her arms and legs, twisting her torso every which way, fighting for purchase on anything solid. He drove her shoulders down, and her heels hit the bottom. Thrashing about, she kept her eyes clamped shut, battling to break free. He released his grip, and she sensed he surged toward the surface. Seizing the moment, she shot upward, blowing out her remaining air. She gasped for breath, coughing and squinting at him bobbing a few feet from her.

There was no room to think, only time to react. *Get out of the water.* Launching back toward the dock, she swam for her life, but he clutched her leg and yanked her back. His grip slipped, but he lunged forward and dunked her under the water. She hit the bottom in the shallower end, and her hands landed behind her on the silty, rock-pocked lakebed. Panicking, she cowered into a ball, drawing her shoulders down. The move loosened his clutch, and for a moment she was free. *Keep fighting. You've got to move.*

She burst up from the bottom to within reach of the ladder. Stretching forward, she grabbed a rung, but before she could tighten her grip, his fist hammered her wrist and severed her hold on the lifeline. *Fight, Liv, fight. Don't do this to Dad. Get an advantage.* After a deep inhale, she dipped down to the bottom, swept her hands through the silt, and grasped a smooth, palm-sized stone. *Strike and follow through.* Then she blasted up through the surface, drew her arm back, and delivered a decisive blow.

CHAPTER 37

Chris lost consciousness with the targeted strike to the side of his neck aimed at his vagus nerve. She had learned the impactful tactic from a self-defense course she had attended two summers ago. Her instinct sprung her toward the ladder, and she footed a rung and clung to a rail, ready to climb. The blow's effects would be merely momentary, granting her a few precious seconds to flee.

She checked over her shoulder with her heart pounding to ensure he wasn't following her. His head rolled to his side and then dipped facedown into the water. *No-no-no. Not you, too.* She didn't hesitate. She leapt from the ladder, lunging for his shoulders, and tipped his chin back. *I just wanted to stun you. I'm not like Jenn.* Her strength and stamina were fading. The adrenaline rush that had fueled her fight no longer cloaked the fatiguing shock of the lake's cold water. She grunted, equally angered and frustrated, knowing there was only one move to make—keep the man who just tried to murder her afloat and swim him back to the shore.

The water's depth dropped as she passed the halfway point along the dock. Faint sirens blared from the park's front side, confirming help was coming. As she got nearer to the shore, Chris bottomed out, and in her exhaustion, she could no longer move him. She wrapped her hands under his shoulders, counted to three, and tried heaving him farther. Her foot slipped, and she flew backward, landing in the water. Scrambling to her feet, she reached for and yanked up his collar.

She rested to catch her breath and wipe her eyes. Chris moaned, and she backed away, wary of him regaining consciousness. His eyes remained shut, and so she stood, lifted his shoulders, and lugged him closer.

"Olivia!" Cole said as he sprinted toward her.

She fully exhaled and tried projecting "help," but all that came was a breathy plea that even she could barely hear.

Cole launched full steam into the lake, and she backed off as he dragged Chris the rest of the way. She staggered out of the water and onto the shore and then doubled over, coughing and gasping for air.

Cole knelt on the ground by Chris as he was coming to. "What happened here?"

She pointed at Chris while watching Preston and Jayden hustle toward them. "He tried to kill me."

Chris opened his eyes and rolled his neck from side to

side. Cole removed a pair of handcuffs from a case on his duty belt and flipped him over onto his stomach.

Jayden rushed over to Olivia and placed a hand on her back. "Easy. Take deep breaths."

She nodded and slowed her rapid, shallow breathing.

"What happened?" Jayden asked.

Cole looked up at Preston, who was standing over Chris. "She says he tried to kill her."

Preston locked on Olivia as Jayden was bracing her upright. "Are you okay?" he asked.

Olivia quickstepped toward him. "Mikey. We have to find him. I think he walked back up the trail that leads to his house." She pointed at the trees where she had last seen him and started in that direction.

He grabbed her shoulder. "Whoa, Olivia. Hold on."

"Come on. Hurry! I had to separate from him. It was the only way. Quick, he can't be far."

"Olivia, stop," Preston said. "He's at his house. He's safe."

She stilled and peered again in the direction she had flung her phone. "Are you sure? He's okay?"

Preston nodded. "Yes. He's fine. He's with Melissa and Kevin."

The relief drained her last bit of energy, and her legs weakened and wobbled.

He took hold of her hand and elbow. "Let's sit you down over there on the bank."

"Preston?" Cole yelled over. "What about him?"

"Call an ambulance for him. For her, too."

She waved off the offer. "No, I'm not injured."

He led her to a grassy patch just off the trail and eased her to the ground. "Sit here and rest until you're steady. Are you sure you're not hurt?"

Not so much hurt as miserably soaked. Her shoulder ached, her palms stung, and she was shivering. "I'm freezing."

He removed his jacket, squatted, and wrapped it around her shoulders. Then he cradled her hands, inspecting the scrapes on her skin, and wiped away some of the dirt and debris. "These need to be cleaned as soon as possible. Who knows what's in that water. You don't want to get an infection."

The warmth and weight of his jacket soothed her senses. Her head cleared, and she gasped, speaking rapid-fire. "Jenn. You have to find her. She killed Dunn." She glanced at Chris, who was now standing with his hands cuffed behind his back. "He said she was leaving for the Netherlands. She may already be gone. The missing vials from the case are in Mikey's pockets."

She tried to scramble to her feet, but Preston grasped her shoulder, grounding her on the grass.

"Hey, Olivia. Look at me. Slow down. Stay down. Please." He waved Jayden over and then locked on Olivia's eyes. "Are you okay sitting here for a few minutes?" She nodded, and he continued, "I'm going to call Kevin, and then you can tell me more about Jenn."

He stood, removed his cell from his pocket, and stepped a few feet away. "Hey, Kevin. We found them down by the lake … yeah, he's in custody … I need you to check Mikey's pockets for the testing vials from Dunn's case." He yelled over to Cole. "Get him out of here." He waited on his phone for another minute. "I'm here. Go ahead … how many? … Okay. I'll send someone up there to collect them." He glanced back at Olivia and lowered his voice. "I'm not sure. Pretty shook up, I think. I'll let you know."

When he had finished his call, Jayden walked over to him and peeked around his side. "Is she alright?"

"EMS will look her over, and we'll see what they say. I need you to go to Melissa's and collect evidence from Kevin. First, though, call into the station and get a BOLO issued for Jennifer Lovelace. She may be outbound on an international flight to the Netherlands. Contact airport security at IAD, DCA, and BWI directly."

"Got it." She pulled out her phone and headed for the trail leading to Melissa's house.

Preston rejoined Olivia as she was getting up from the ground and removing his jacket. "Keep it on," he said. "Let's go back to my truck and get the heat started. EMS will clean those cuts and give you a once-over."

She was too tired to protest, and besides, his plan sounded on point. He steadied her, keeping an arm wrapped around her shoulder as they walked back to the front side. She was soaked and shivering, but the warmth of his body next to hers felt good, and she wasn't about to protest that either.

When they reached the parking lot, he led her straight to his truck. She slid into the passenger side, and he started the engine, blasting the heat and turning on the seat warmer.

"This should help while we're waiting for EMS," he said.

She nodded, keeping his jacket wrapped tightly around her. "I'm already warming up. I do love a heated seat."

"Sit tight. As soon as I finish what I need to and the paramedics look you over, I'll drive you to the station so we can get a statement. I'll take you home after."

She leaned her head back against the seat. "My car is at Melissa's."

"Where's your key?"

She reached into her pocket, retrieving the fob.

"That won't work anymore. Do you have a spare?"

"At my house. I'll call my dad to bring it."

"Don't bother with it tonight. It'll be late by the time we're done. You can come for it tomorrow. I'll let Melissa know. I'm sure she won't mind. I'll take you home after we're done at the station." He opened his door and got out.

She brushed mud from her hands, and then combed her fingers through her drying, tangled hair. She leaned sideways toward the driver's seat. "Can I borrow your phone to call my dad? I better tell him what happened before I show up looking like a swamp creature."

He grinned and ducked back into the cab, handing

her his cell. "I don't think you look like that at all." He grabbed a bottle of water from the door well and placed it in the center console's cupholder. "I'm sure you're thirsty. There's another in the backseat if you want more."

"You're too kind to me, Detective."

"Take your time. We're going to be here for a while. I'll check in on you in a few minutes." He backed out and closed the door.

Her breathing calmed as her heart warmed, watching him walk away. She snuggled in his jacket, softened into the leather seat, and allowed her body to ease. She closed her eyes and rested in the silence, remembering Maria's advice—the only certainty in life is change.

CHAPTER 38

Olivia woke up at her leisure Friday morning, still drained from yesterday's trauma. Last night, she had been at the police station until eleven, providing her statement and answering all of Preston's questions. When she returned home, she had first gone up to shower, and then rehashed the harrowing story for over an hour with her father.

She rolled toward the nightstand and grabbed her cell, checking the time through the shattered screen. She had missed a pair of calls and two texts. Sophia had phoned twice this morning, and then followed up with a message, responding to the voice mail Olivia had left her late last night. The message read: "Are you okay? Call me ASAP."

She responded with a thumbs-up emoji and "Will call or see you soon." Feeling an ache in her left shoulder, she rotated it forward and back and then pulled aside the neckline of her T-shirt to view the dark purple bruise from her tumble. *Unbelievable. I had to rescue Chris. I could've died. I don't think I'll ever walk out on that dock again. Maybe not even go to the lake. Pools are out indefinitely.*

The second text was from Daniel: "Have a great weekend. Thinking of you." She eyed the plush Texas Ranger teddy bear propped against the nightstand table lamp, recalling her walk with Preston from the lake to his truck yesterday afternoon. She scrolled through and reread Daniel's recent messages. All his words had become distorted through the fractured glass. There was no need to respond or tell him anything about what had happened. Those who mattered now already knew.

Soft, rhythmic snoring emanated from the foot of her bed. She glanced toward her half-opened door and then peered over the mattress' edge at her loyal sidekick. Buddy was napping with his head resting on the bottom corner of the cozy duvet. "You had a late night, too. Were you standing guard, little bud?" She quietly rose and walked to her dresser, not wanting to stir him from his restful slumber.

She slipped on a fleece robe over her T-shirt and navy pajama pants. Her father was speaking with someone by the front door, but by the time she peeked over the hallway banister, the visitor already had left. She went back into her room and polished off her morning look with a ponytail and a pair of socks, hoping two cups of strong coffee would inspire a more stylish outfit.

Her father closed the newspaper as she joined him in

the kitchen. He glanced up, doing a double take. "Good morning. You look, ah ..."

"Frightful?" she offered.

"No. I would never say such a thing about my daughter."

She slid a chair away from the table and plopped down. "But you would think it."

He scooted back and stood. "I'll get you some coffee. Looks like you could use it."

She laid her arms and head on the woven cotton, cornflower-blue place mat in front of her.

"Did you sleep at all?" he asked.

She nodded without lifting her head. "I think I slept the whole night through without moving. Who was here earlier? I heard you talking to someone."

He opened the refrigerator. "Do you want the almond stuff or real milk?"

"Almond, thanks."

"Preston came by. He and Bert brought your car back." He turned and placed the mug in front of her. "How about something to eat? I can make bacon and eggs."

She straightened and spooned sweetener into her coffee. "How'd they do that?"

"Last night, when you got back and went up to shower, Preston asked me for your spare key. He said he would bring your car here this morning. What do you say to some breakfast? We have sausage."

She cradled the steaming mug, allowing it to warm

her hands. Buddy ambled into the kitchen, sniffed near the stove, and then lay on the welcome mat.

"Sweetie? How about something to eat?"

"Not now. I swear I can still taste the lake water. I know I swallowed some of it. I brushed my teeth three times last night and must've used a quarter of a bottle of mouthwash."

"You know what would be good for that? Gargling with salt water."

She shook her head and grinned. "That's your answer to everything."

"It works. Don't knock it until you try it. Maybe you should see a doctor."

She sipped her coffee. "Yesterday, the paramedics told me what I should watch out for. They said I'd probably be fine, but it's possible something in the water may cause an infection. If I develop a rash or fever …" She paused and cringed. "Or experience gastrointestinal distress, then I should see a doctor. With my luck, if I get any of those, I bet I know which one it'll be."

"I'll stop by the store and pick up a twelve-pack of ginger ale for you, just in case. Any concerns about you growing another finger?"

She splayed her hands, checking her skin. "I didn't dive into toxic waste. At least, I hope not. I feel okay. I'm just tired."

"You should take it easy today. How about giving yourself a week before you get involved in the next murder we have around here."

She slid the vase of calla lilies and lavender closer to her. She rearranged a few of the stems and then repositioned the bouquet at the center of the table beside the bowl of Jack Be Little pumpkins. "No, I'm done. That's all in the past. It's behind me."

He patted her shoulder. "I'm all in for that. No more sleuthing."

She nodded. "Wholeheartedly agree, unless—"

"I don't want to hear unless anything." He pulled Buddy's leash off the key rack. "Do you want me to bring you some lunch? I can run by Jillian's. I know you like her sandwiches."

"No, thanks. I'm going into town for the Halloween festival. I promised Tori I would come and see Tyler in the costume parade."

"Do you want me to drive you there?"

"Not necessary. I'm not planning on staying long. I think I will grab a bite to eat here, and then clean up and leave in about an hour. You go ahead, take Buddy for his walk."

He donned his fleece jacket. "He's the one taking me for my walk. Come on, Buddy. Let's get this over with." He clipped the leash to the dog's collar, and then they left through the kitchen.

She made a bowl of oatmeal, tossing in a handful of slivered almonds and blueberries for pep. After she ate and downed a second cup of coffee, she cleaned up, changed clothes, and gathered what she needed.

She pushed open the porch screen and was pulling

the front door shut to lock up and leave when Jason turned his pickup into the driveway. She watched as he stopped a car's length behind her Expedition. He opened his door and hopped out, bypassing any conventional greeting. He stepped to the truck's rear, heaved a white Styrofoam cooler out of the bed, and placed it on the ground.

She slowly descended the porch steps and warily walked toward him, having no clue what was happening. "Jason, I didn't expect to see you today. Here, at my house, again. I was on my way out though …"

He leaned down, lifted the cooler's lid, and removed a white plastic garbage bag. He stepped forward, thrusting the bag toward her, and she reflexively grabbed it, as one does when being handed something suspicious by a practical stranger. The unexpected heft pulled her arm down, and the bag landed on the ground.

"That's a twenty-pound turkey," he said. "It's all cleaned and ready for the oven. It's the freshest and tastiest bird you'll ever eat. Better than anything store-bought. Do you want me to carry it inside for you?"

She lifted the bag, needing both hands to raise it. "No, thanks. I'll manage. But I don't understand. Why are you giving me this?"

"To thank you for what you did for Melissa and Mikey." He repositioned the lid, hoisted the cooler from the ground, and placed it back in the truck's bed.

She was at a loss for what to say. Of all the possibilities she thought the day may bring, she hadn't accounted for this one. The bag's weight strained her grip, so she rested the turkey on the ground as her manners returned to her. "Jason, thank you. We'll enjoy it."

"If you ever need anything, you know where to find me." He got into his truck and backed down the drive. She watched as he left, and then she stood for a minute more, staring at the bagged bird by her feet, feeling no need to question it.

"Alright then. Looks like it'll be an early Thanksgiving." She picked up her gift and hauled it into the house. She swapped the dirty bag for a clean roaster pan and stashed the turkey in the refrigerator, making a mental list of the ingredients she needed for her corn bread stuffing.

CHAPTER 39

The town square brimmed with spirit and chatter as pint-sized zombies, mummies, and ghosts scurried along the trick-or-treating trail, collecting candy in plastic pumpkins. There was no official start time for the parade. The children could begin whenever they arrived and circle the route as many times as they pleased. Most, though, had enough after one go-around and ditched their loot with their parents so that they could frolic on the moon bounce and play the carnival games.

Moms and dads watched their parading kiddos from the sidelines while sitting on hay bales and sipping spiced cider. Food vendors had parked their trucks along one end of the square and were fanning out the seductive aroma of kettle corn and funnel cakes to reel in customers. The sun shone bright in the autumnal blue sky, and though today was perfect sweater weather, the crisp fall air hinted a change in season was on its way.

Olivia spotted A.J. and Sophia sitting next to each other on a hay bale near one corner of the square. She strolled over to greet them while passing a trio of vampires, a bumblebee, and a waving slice of blueberry pie.

A.J. stood and hugged her as Sophia whacked her arm. "I could kill you," Sophia said. "What were you thinking? You need to be cloistered to keep out of trouble."

Olivia raised one eyebrow. "That's a negative, Ghost Rider."

A.J. kept his arm around her shoulders. "Are you okay? How come I have to hear about what happened to you from Soph?"

"Excuse me, I'm her best friend. She's obligated to tell me first."

He jabbed his thumb at his chest. "I've known her longer."

"I apologize to both of you. I was exhausted last night, and I knew I would be seeing you today."

"The real question is, why do we even need to be going through this type of thing with you again?" Sophia said.

Because Preston was right. Mikey was saying something in his drawing, and I wasn't about to sit idly by if there was a threat to anyone I know.

A.J. nodded. "Yeah, Liv. What she said."

I'd do it all again in a heartbeat. She deflected the question, teasing him. "Really? Because you didn't seem to mind so much last time."

He held his hands up, surrendering and abandoning any further admonishment. "Okay. Truce then. Seriously, are you alright? Shouldn't you be at home resting? Soph and I were planning to come over to your house after we helped her mom and grandmother set up their table for the bake sale and said hi to Tori and Tyler when they arrive."

"I just have a bruise on my shoulder and scrapes on my hands. I'm mostly tired, and my lower back is sore. I think I tweaked a muscle when I was heaving Chris out of the lake."

A.J. clasped her hand. "Come, take a load off."

She gingerly settled on the hay bale, and though she wouldn't mistake it for memory foam, being off her feet eased the tension in her lower back.

"Liv!" Tori sauntered over, pushing an adaptive stroller from the sidewalk onto the grass. Tyler sat huddled inside dressed in a full, fuzzy koala bear suit. His hands and feet had morphed into paws, and saucer-sized ears flopped down on his cheeks.

Olivia couldn't help but to giggle as she pulled her phone out of her pocket. "Tori, he's adorable. I need a picture. Where's your costume?"

Tori sighed as Olivia lined up a portrait shot. "I didn't have time to get dressed. Turns out it takes longer than I thought to wrangle a toddler into a getup like this." She reached down and rubbed the top of the koala head that fully encircled his face. "Especially this tater tot."

Tyler clapped and snickered. "Ta-ta-ta!"

Tori leaned forward and kissed his rosy cheek. "That's right, you're a little tater ta-ta."

"Ta-ta-ta!" He reached forward for Olivia's hand, but the chest harness restricted his movement and kept him securely in the stroller.

She grabbed his fingers instead and then gave him a high five. "You're the cutest koala I've ever seen." She glanced up at Tori. "Were you supposed to be mama koala?"

Tori parked the stroller alongside the hay bale and then plunked down next to Olivia. "Not quite. I was all in on the Aussie theme, though. I ordered an authentic Crocodile Hunter uniform straight from the Australia Zoo. I'm still totally going to wear it for gardening. It's surprisingly practical."

"Crikey," Olivia joked.

"I'll buy you one, too. Seems appropriate for this wild and crazy life you're leading now. Last night, I received this weird text from Soph about you almost being killed —again." She glanced up at Sophia. "By the way, your middle-of-the-night panic texts are completely incomprehensible. Then, I saw the paper posted on their website this morning that the police arrested Chris in connection with the murder at the lake. So, would somebody please explain to me what happened?"

Olivia scooted over, making room for Sophia to sit,

and then recounted the skeleton outline of events, unsure of how much she was at liberty to tell.

Tori tucked back one of Tyler's koala ears that had flopped down over his eyes. "So, Jenn's in custody, then?"

"Yes. Right before Preston drove me home—"

"That was nice of him," Tori said with a wink. "Please continue."

"The water shorted my key fob's battery, so I had to leave my Expedition at Melissa's, and he offered to—"

"Of course he did. Just saying, he seems handy to have around. Please, continue."

"Anyway. The state police spotted Jenn's car on Route 28, near the exit for Dulles Airport. Turns out, she wasn't outbound to the Netherlands, like Chris said. She had a one-way ticket to Taiwan."

"Why the heck Taiwan?" A.J. asked.

"Preston told me last night it was probably because Taiwan doesn't have an extradition treaty with the U.S. It's an odd, but useful fact, if you ever have the need. Jenn said to me that the only time she had been overseas was when she attended a conference in East Asia, so she has some familiarity with the area.

"Wow, Liv," Tori quipped. "This keeps getting better. A flight from justice. You could write a book about this. So, then what happened?"

"That's all I know."

"I don't understand," Tori said. "Why did she do it?"

"I'm not sure. Chris told me it was an accident. But

there had to be something about those samples Dunn had collected that would tie back to Fields Farm."

"How horrible for his parents," Sophia said. "For Kevin, too. It must be devastating. I wonder if they'll still go through with the sale."

"I'd be shocked if they do," Olivia replied. "I think, business-wise, they'll probably want to distance themselves from Chris as far as possible. If the investigation finds the farm has violated regulations for organic practices, there'll be hefty fines. It's a mess. I imagine they'll hold on to the property until they can deal with the legal repercussions of what Chris and Jenn did."

Sophia nudged Olivia's side. "All of this makes me grateful for the family and friends I have. Speaking of which, do you think you'll be up to coming tomorrow for our Día de los Muertos celebration at my parents' house? We'll honor our family there and then drive to the cemetery afterwards. We'll be at Saint Luke's about one o'clock. A.J.'s bringing Paige's mom."

"Count me in," Tori said.

Olivia nodded. "I'll be at both." She glanced over Sophia's shoulder at Preston standing a short distance from them on the sidewalk, scanning the crowd across the town square. She popped up, ignoring the twinge in her back, and then stepped on and over the hay bale. "Save my spot and make room for Sam. She'll be joining us. I'll be back in a minute."

CHAPTER 40

Preston offered a friendly wave and a tip of his Stetson as Olivia maneuvered around a princess and a rug rat linebacker wearing an oversized football helmet and shoulder pads. "How are you feeling this morning?" he asked.

She straightened her posture, hoping she hadn't been slouching. "A little tired."

"I bet. You've been through a horrible ordeal. Going back in the water after Chris like that was something not many people would do. That's highly commendable."

"Thanks, but had I died, my actions probably would've seemed stupid. I couldn't let him drown, though. I just reacted in the moment, but it was the right decision. Had he died by my hands … I know it was self-defense, but still, that's not something I wanted to live with for the rest of my life."

He nodded without taking his focus off her. "Saving someone's life is never an act of stupidity."

She felt his steady gaze and suddenly regretted wearing her faded jeans and pilled sweatshirt. Twisting her back slightly, she gently stretched her aching muscles. "Oh, that feels good. I think I tweaked something in my back. I feel like I'm running on empty this morning even after two cups of coffee. I'm sure you had a longer night than me, though."

He pointed to a bench. "You want to sit down?"

"No, I'm good for now. Thanks for the offer. You probably didn't get much sleep yourself."

He scrunched his nose as his lips parted with a thin smile. "Does it show?"

"No, I didn't mean it like that. You look great—I mean for probably being up all night." She hoped that didn't sound as awkward to him as it did to her.

His dimple showed through his short-stubbled beard. "Thanks, I think. You're right. It was a late night. The state police took Jenn to the Loudoun County Detention Center. After I dropped you off at your father's, I drove up there and questioned her."

"And then you brought my car to the house this morning? You didn't have to do that. It could've waited, but I'm grateful. That seems above and beyond your duty."

He brushed off the compliment with a quick head-shake. "I wanted to. I promised your father that I would return it as soon as I could."

"And you always keep your promises, right?"

"Something like that."

She glanced at the inn. "I bet that's your mother's influence."

"My dad's too. But it's true I would never hear the end of it from her if she knew I went back on my word, especially to you. I just wanted it to be one less thing you had to worry about today."

She reflexively lowered her gaze as her cheeks warmed, hating that she always blushed so easily. *You're flattering yourself, Liv.* She couldn't deny her attraction to him, but after what had happened with Daniel, she didn't fully trust her judgment regarding a man's intentions. Preston had no pretense about him and always had her best interest in mind. But she didn't know whether the doubt was about misreading their chemistry or reluctance to risk her heart again. *I don't know if I'm ready.* She looked up and changed the subject to something less complicated. "Did you find anything out from Jenn last night?"

His eyes narrowed with inquiry. "Is this still a story you're working on?"

She shook her head adamantly. "No. My part of the story is over."

"Off the record, then?"

She nodded. "Completely."

A mother rushed toward them on the sidewalk, holding the hands of two tyke-sized werewolves. He waited until they passed by and then checked all around, ensuring no one was within earshot.

His smile faded as he dropped into detective mode.

"Chris said that Kevin had initially contacted him and Jenn about the bloom. Kevin asked that she look at it on account of her background, and then advise him whether it seemed serious enough to report to the VDEQ Jenn called the VDEQ herself and arranged to meet Dunn on Monday. Apparently, he got there early, and that's when you saw him. Chris said she had collected uncontaminated water from elsewhere in the lake and had planned to swap it with whatever samples Dunn took."

"She'd been lying from the start," Olivia said. "Why would she take her own samples?"

"She was afraid of what Dunn's samples may show. Chris said she had been using an experimental fertilizer on the farm's back fields. It was something she was researching, but it's not EPA approved. She was worried that some may have leached into the water table and worked its way into the lake. They schemed to divert attention away from the farm by accusing the country club."

Olivia subtly picked off several strands of Buddy's hair from her sweatshirt and let them float to the ground, hoping he didn't notice. "Chris' tirade when I was there speaking with Philip and Ben must've been part of the show. Yell loud enough so others can hear, and that's how rumors start and go viral."

"That's for sure," he concurred. "Whispering Meadows was an easy target because of their EPA violations last year. I don't understand all the science, but the samples Dunn took might've raised a red flag, pointing to the farm as the source of the bloom because of the nature of the contaminants. I'm sure that would've nixed the sale."

"No doubt. Goodbye jackpot payday. So, what they were using was both illegal and in violation of the regulations. But why kill him?"

"According to Chris, she was there when Dunn was collecting his samples, and she attempted to swap the vials when he was documenting his findings. He saw what she was doing and tried to grab the vials from her. She panicked, and there was some sort of struggle. He fell off the dock and hit his head on the kayak."

Olivia raised her eyebrows "She left him to drown? That's stone cold."

He pursed his lips and nodded. "Looks that way. Jenn took his testing kit—"

"That was the box on the dock," Olivia said.

"Come again?"

She gestured as if holding Mikey's drawing in her hand while tracing her finger across the page. "We first thought that he drew me twice—when I was there with A.J. and then when I found Dunn. It looked like the same two-armed stick figure, so it seemed to fit. But the figure on the dock wasn't me. It was Jenn with the testing kit. He must've been close by to see where she had stashed it."

He nodded as if slowly buying into her theory.

"Okay, that makes sense, but what about the figure behind the tree?"

"Two arms, two legs. Just like A.J. when he was walking with me. Just like Dunn, dead in the water. I bet Mikey would draw all men with four limbs, but women with just two arms. Dollars to doughnuts—our mystery man was Jason. We know he was collecting pinecones with Mikey about the time I found Dunn. And then Mikey got ahead of Jason on the trail when he was busting up that turkey trap in the woods. The other four-legged figure by the dock—it was smaller than the one we assumed was Buddy, so it could've been something like a squirrel."

Preston rubbed his chin. "You remembered all of those details just from seeing his drawing once?"

She shrugged, smiling innocently. "Photographic memory." *Via cell phone.*

"Really? I'll have to be more careful around you then. That all seems to check out. She hid the case and planned to come back later to retrieve it."

"But Mikey moved it," Olivia added. "Jenn didn't hesitate to pick up the kit when Buddy found it. I bet she was eager to have a plausible explanation for why her prints were all over it."

He nodded. "That's a reasonable conclusion. We matched her prints in the system from an arrest she had a few years back from taking part in an illegal demonstration. Had we discovered the case first and tested it for prints, we would've identified her immediately."

"She was so close to getting away with it, but she got sloppy. Not so smart after all. Did she admit to any of this?"

"No. She lawyered up. Didn't say a word, other than blaming Chris for everything."

Olivia shook her head out of disgust and disbelief. "I bet. What a sweet pea. Till death or criminal charges do we part. After questioning them both, do you believe him?"

He readjusted his hat, setting it firmly on his head with the brim tilted just above his engaging, cognac-brown eyes. "I'm leaning that way. He's cooperating. He provided enough details during the interrogation last night to get a search warrant for the farm. He told us where we could find records and the compounds they were using. He was adamant that neither his parents nor Kevin knew anything about what he was doing with Jenn. We have two deputies over there now, collecting evidence. There's a lot to untangle."

"What a pair—a real Bonnie and Clyde. Safe to say the wedding is off. Your mother will be disappointed that she won't be hosting a rehearsal dinner."

A young father walked by with his son dressed as a Canadian Mountie.

"Oh, look," she said. "He could be your newest recruit."

He chuckled. "We like to start them early."

She glanced behind her at the hay bales. Tori was pushing Tyler's stroller toward the starting line of the

Halloween parade route. Sam had arrived and was chatting with A.J. and Sophia.

She turned back toward him. "Well, I guess the mystery is solved then." The conversation seemed to have run its course, but she didn't want it to end. The background chatter faded, and she lingered, scrambling for something to say. "Feel free to say no, but tomorrow we're all meeting at St. Luke's. Soph's family is honoring Paige as part of their Día de los Muertos celebration. I know you said you would be there with your mother, so if you want to stop by, we'll be there around one o'clock. I'm sure everybody would be glad to see you. And then we could all go together to your father's and my mother's grave, too."

He casually dipped his fingers into his pockets, easing his stance. "That's kind of you to ask, and sounds nice. We'd be happy to join you. I didn't know your mother was buried there. I knew your father lived alone before you came back, but I wasn't sure what the situation was."

"Completely understandable. It's a story for another day."

"Well then, I'll look forward to hearing it if you ever want to share. Listen, I know my mother invited you and your father to dinner tomorrow night at the inn. Please don't feel obligated. You know her."

"We'd be happy to come. Good food, charming ambiance, and delightful company. What's not to love? We'll see you at seven." Having her dad with her gave her a safety net. It was just another dinner with Preston and his mother. No pressure and nothing at stake. *Indeed, what's not to love.*

"Great," he said. "It's a date—oh, sorry that came out wrong." He grimaced and bowed his head. "I didn't mean like a date-date. That's not what I meant at all. And that didn't come out right either. It's not that I wouldn't—"

She held up her hand to stop him before he put his foot any deeper into his mouth. "No worries. I know what you meant, and I'm looking forward to it." *More than you know.* She glanced at the ground and tucked her hair behind her ears, thinking it was now best to pick this all back up tomorrow before she likewise embarrassed herself with a slip of the tongue. "I guess I should let you return to your duty before I find myself locked up again for interfering with official police business. With all these ghouls and gremlins running amuck, you never know what manner of mayhem may ensue. Apple Station— thrills and chills around every corner, right? I'm going to watch Tori and Tyler circle the trick-or-treating trail and then head on home for some R and R."

"Take it easy today, and if there's anything I can help you with, call me. Don't hesitate." He grinned, gesturing toward the square. "But what about the parade? You're not going to take a lap around? Pick up some treats to take home? You deserve it after all you've been through."

She shook her head, matching his playful tone. "That candy they give out over there … child's play. I happen to possess highly classified intel on who really gives out the best chocolate. Besides, my costume-wearing days are long over. No masks for me. I am who I am. What you see is what you get."

His smile doubled as they held each other's eyes. "I can live with that."

They said their goodbyes, and she set off back to join A.J., Sophia, and Sam in watching Tori and Tyler trek around the Halloween trail. Days like this was why she had remained in Apple Station. She had come home six months ago, feeling disconnected and about to embark on a life that would've taken her even farther from the supports she needed. Though her long-term plans were still unclear, they now didn't involve keeping one foot in the past. Tomorrow, she would celebrate the lives of those that had gone before her with her friends and family. It would be a day full of joy and gratitude for the good times and memories they shared. Then she would dine with someone who may be a part of her future. There was no need to overthink or put undue pressure on this potential new beginning. She released her past with Daniel without a word and now embraced the unknown, allowing the feelings she held silently in her heart to say the most.

The End

ACKNOWLEDGMENTS

I'm deeply grateful for all those who have supported me in the writing of this book.

Thank you to my brilliant editor Serena Clarke for making this story shine. Your encouragement, guidance, and support are appreciated beyond words. Thank you to my wonderful proofreader LaVerne Clark for having my back and being my last line of defense. Thank you to Robin Vuchnich for your exquisite cover art. Your design brings a smile to my heart.

Thank you to the welcoming and supportive communities of Sisters in Crime and the James River Writers.

In memory of my parents ... with much gratitude ... to my mom, who always made sure I had plenty of pens and paper to write my stories, and to my dad, who always encouraged me and whose biggest hope was that someday I'd be writing books. *I did it Dad!*

A special heartfelt thank you to Marcy Sebek and Lynn Fahnesstock for your support and guidance. I will always be grateful.

Thank you to my husband for all the years, support, and laughter. My love always.

THANK YOU FOR READING

Thank you for reading *Silence Says the Most*. I'm deeply grateful for all the support that readers like you have shown for *The Olivia Penn Mystery Series*. If you enjoyed this book, could you do me a favor and leave a brief review on the retailer of your choice?

Reviews make a massive difference in helping me to connect with more readers and support my ability to continue writing these stories for you. Thank you!

ALSO BY KATHLEEN BAILEY

Where the Light Shines Through

Made in the USA
Monee, IL
29 November 2022

19010441R00177